THE IRRESISTIBLE BUCK

Barbara Cartland

Barbara Cartland Ebooks Ltd

This edition © 2020

ISBNs

9781788673501   EPUB

9781788673518   PAPERBACK

Book design by M-Y Books
m-ybooks.co.uk

THE BARBARA CARTLAND ETERNAL COLLECTION

The Barbara Cartland Eternal Collection is the unique opportunity to collect all five hundred of the timeless beautiful romantic novels written by the world's most celebrated and enduring romantic author.

Named the Eternal Collection because Barbara's inspiring stories of pure love, just the same as love itself, the books will be published on the internet at the rate of four titles per month until all five hundred are available.

The Eternal Collection, classic pure romance available worldwide for all time .

THE LATE DAME BARBARA CARTLAND

Barbara Cartland, who sadly died in May 2000 at the grand age of ninety eight, remains one of the world's most famous romantic novelists. With worldwide sales of over one billion, her outstanding 723 books have been translated into thirty six different languages, to be enjoyed by readers of romance globally.

Writing her first book 'Jigsaw' at the age of 21, Barbara became an immediate bestseller. Building upon this initial success, she wrote continuously throughout her life, producing bestsellers for an astonishing 76 years. In addition to Barbara Cartland's legion of fans in the UK and across Europe, her books have always been immensely popular in the USA. In 1976 she achieved the unprecedented feat of having books at numbers 1 & 2 in the prestigious B. Dalton Bookseller bestsellers list.

Although she is often referred to as the 'Queen of Romance', Barbara Cartland also wrote several historical biographies, six autobiographies and numerous theatrical plays as well as books on life, love, health and cookery. Becoming one of Britain's most popular media personalities and dressed in her trademark pink, Barbara spoke on radio and television about social and political issues, as well as making many public appearances.

In 1991 she became a Dame of the Order of the British Empire for her contribution to literature and her work for humanitarian and charitable causes.

Known for her glamour, style, and vitality Barbara Cartland became a legend in her own lifetime. Best remembered for her wonderful romantic novels and loved by millions of readers worldwide, her books remain treasured for their heroic heroes, plucky heroines and traditional values. But above all, it was Barbara Cartland's overriding belief in the positive power of love to help, heal and improve the quality of life for everyone that made her truly unique.

CHAPTER ONE
1802

Lord Melburne yawned.

As he did so, he realised that he was not tired but bored, bored with the picture of fat cupids discreetly veiled that faced him over the mantelshelf, bored as well with the pink satin curtains festooned with silk bows and tassels and bored too with the over-scented overheated room itself.

His eyes lit on his coat of superfine blue cloth thrown over the chair and his white muslin cravat lying negligently amongst the bottles, lotions, salves and perfumes on the overcrowded dressing table.

And the boredom of realising that he must rise and put them on made him yawn again.

"*Tu es fatigué, mon cher?*" came a soft voice from beside him.

He looked sideways to see two dark eyes raised to his, two red lips pouting provocatively and knew that they also bored him.

It was indeed an unfortunate moment for his Lordship to discover that he was bored with his mistress. Lying beside him against the lace-frilled pillows, she was wearing only a ruby necklace, on which he had expended quite an exorbitant sum of money, and red satin slippers to match the stones.

He recalled almost incredulously that he had pursued her ardently only a month ago. It had undoubtedly added some piquancy to his wooing that the lady in question,

Mademoiselle Liane Defroy, was hesitating over whether to accept the protection of the Marquis of Crawley or that of Sir Henry Stainer.

The Marquis might have a higher social position, but Sir Henry Stainer was undoubtedly the wealthier. Both were generous to an extreme, both were members of the much-vaunted set of Corinthians that circled round the Prince of Wales and were *habitués* of Carlton House, the Prince's majestic home in London.

That Lord Melburne had filched Liane from under their aristocratic noses had not only given him a quiet satisfaction but had also made the Prince laugh uproariously and declare that he was irresistible when it came to the fair sex.

It was this irresistibility, Lord Melburne thought now with a frown between his eyes that made life so incredibly boring. The chase was all too short and then the conquest was all too monotonous.

He found himself wishing that he was back with his Regiment and that there were battles still to be fought and won with an endless stream of Frenchmen to be chased and killed. The *damned* Armistice, he complained, had restored him to civilian life and all he could say was that it now seemed cursed dull.

He made a movement to rise and Liane's little hands fluttered towards him.

"*Non, non*!" she exclaimed. "Do not move. It is still very early, and we have so much to say, *tu comprends*!"

Her lips were very near to his. He was overwhelmingly aware of the heavy scent that she used, which he thought was far too sweet, too sickly and now only added to his feelings of distaste.

He seemed almost to shake himself free from her clinging arms as he rose to his feet.

"I must get to bed early," he said, reaching for his cravat. "I am leaving for the country tomorrow."

"For ze country?" Liane repeated, her voice rising a little. "But then why? Why are you leaving me alone? *C'est la folie!* London is very gay, there is so much, how you say, *pour t'amuser.* Why should you wish to go where there is only ze mud?"

His Lordship next fixed his cravat with the experienced hand of a man who can dress competently without the help of a valet.

"I have to see an old friend of my father's," he replied. "I should have gone last week, but you persuaded me, Liane, against my better judgement to stay on in London. Now I must do my duty.

"*C'est impossible!*" Liane protested, sitting up on the bed with the rubies round her neck flashing in the light of the candles. "Have you forgotten ze party tomorrow night, ze party to which we are all invited, *tout le Corps de Ballet?* It will be very gay and I think also very naughty. You will enjoy it."

"I have my doubts about that," Lord Melburne responded, shrugging himself into his coat.

He stood for a moment looking down at her with her long hair dark as a raven's wing that fell below her waist, at the small piquant face with its tip-tilted nose and wide mouth, which had seemed so entrancing only a few weeks ago. She was actually a clever dancer and she exploited her few talents very skilfully.

But he wondered now as he looked at her how he had ever endured the banality of her conversation, the artificial flutterings of her hands, the shrugging of her thin shoulders and the coquettish way that she would veil her eyes with her long mascaraed lashes and contrive to appear mysterious.

There was in fact no mystery, Lord Melburne had discovered.

She looked up at him now, noting almost automatically how handsome he was and how outstanding even in a room full of other good-looking and well bred men.

It was not only his looks, she thought, as so many women had thought before her, that were so attractive, it was not only the squareness of his jaw or those strange grey eyes, which seemed so uncannily penetrating that a woman felt, when he looked at her, that he searched for something deeper than mere surface attraction.

No, Liane perceived with a sudden understanding, it was the cynical lines running from nose to mouth, the twist of his lips that somehow seemed to sneer at life even in moments of enjoyment and the sudden twinkle in his eyes, which belied that very sneer when one least expected it.

Yes, he was irresistible and with a smile she held out her arms towards him.

"Don't linger in ze country," she said softly, "I wait for you, *mon brave. C'est ce que tu desires, n'est-ce pas?*"

"I am not – certain," Lord Melburne replied slowly and, even as he spoke the words, he realised that he had made a mistake –

The scene that followed was noisy, unpleasant and yet inevitable. He left Liane sobbing hysterically on the pillows and wondered as he went down the narrow staircase why he could never end an affair as neatly as other men of his acquaintance did. When they parted from their mistresses it was easy, a mere question of money and perhaps a diamond or two, and there was no ill will.

With him it always meant tears and recriminations, protestations and then the inevitable plaintive,

"What have I done?

"Why do I not attract you anymore?"

"Is there someone else?"

He knew the questions only too well and they were all too familiar.

As he let himself out by the elegant yellow-painted front door and slammed it behind him so that the polished brass knocker went *rat-rat*, he told himself that this was the last time he would be such a fool as to set his mistress up in a house of her own.

It was fashionable to have an opera dancer under one's protection, to take her driving in the Park, to provide her with her own carriage and pair, to expect her to remain ostensibly faithful until the liaison came to an end.

But where this termination proved amicable and uncomplicated where other men were concerned, Lord Melburne was invariably different.

He found himself pursued by clouds of tears and broken-hearted letters, with pleas for an explanation and an almost obstinate refusal to believe that he was no longer interested in her.

His carriage was waiting, the discreet closed carriage he used at night for such visits. The coachman had looked surprised at seeing his Lordship so early and lifted the reins with a jerk.

The smart footman, having closed the carriage door after his Lordship, sprang back onto the box and said out of the corner of his mouth,

"Bet you that's ended!"

"Can't be," the coachman answered. "'E ain't been with 'er more than a month."

"It be ended though," the footman said confidently. "I knows the look on his Nibs's face when 'e says finish and finish it be."

"Never did care for those Frenchies," the coachman remarked. "The one 'e 'ad before last, 'er be an English mort. Now she's a real high-stepper."

"'E were tired of her within three months," the footman said with relish. "I wonder what makes 'im tire so easy."

Inside the coach his Lordship was asking just the same thing. Why did he suddenly and usually unexpectedly find a woman no longer attractive?

He had enjoyed parading Liane in front of his friends. He had taken her to the gaming halls, to the *Albany Rooms*, to *Mott's* and Vauxhall Gardens. It had seemed to him that she outshone every other woman in such places. She was gay, she was amusing, she had a *joie de vivre* and a vitality that galvanised everyone who spoke with her.

"You are a damned lucky fellow," Sir Henry Stainer had said to Lord Melburne and the envy in his friend's voice had been most gratifying.

He wondered now if Sir Henry would stoop to pick up his leavings. But if it were not Stainer, there would be more than a dozen others only too willing to vie for the favours of the Frenchwoman who had captivated the fancy of quite a number of the most fastidious and spoilt young bloods of the *Beau Ton*.

'And yet I no longer want her,' Lord Melburne thought.

He stretched out his legs so that they rested across to the seat opposite.

"To hell with it!" he said aloud. "To hell with all women!"

He knew it was absurd that he should be feeling slightly guilty over the scene that had just taken place. He knew too that it was Liane and not he who was breaking the rules.

The arrangement between a gentleman and his mistress was supposed to be entirely a commercial agreement. They enjoyed each other's company, it was a woman's job to be as fascinating as possible and to extort by every means she could think of the maximum amount of payment for her favours.

But there was never supposed to be any question of love, heartthrobs or hurt feelings.

And yet where Buck Melburne was concerned the rules always went by the board. He had been called 'Buck' since he was only a little boy. Even his relations had difficulty in remembering what were his real names.

It was a nickname he acquired after he appeared for the first time in a suit of satin knee breeches and he managed even at the age of six to wear them with an air that brought the exclamation from one of his father's friends,

"Gad, he looks like a Buck already!"

The name had stuck and there was no doubt that it was most appropriate. The Prince of Wales followed the fashions he set with his plain well-cut coats and exquisitely tied cravats, his dislike of ostentatious jewellery or anything that pertained to the Dandy Set.

And the name was appropriate for other reasons as there was no one in the whole country who could tool a coach or a phaeton so skilfully and he had a far better seat than any of his contemporaries when he rode to hounds. He could shoot more accurately and box with an almost professional skill.

Buck Melburne was the most sought after, the most envied and the most irresistible man in London.

It was, however, with the lines of cynicism engraved deep on his face and his mouth set in a hard line that his Lordship stepped out of his carriage in Berkeley Square and entered the hall of his London house.

He handed his hat and cane to the butler.

"I shall leave for Melburne at half after nine o'clock tomorrow morning, Smithson," he said. "Order my high perch phaeton and tell Hawkins to go ahead of me in the luggage cart. The fast one, not that Noah's Ark he tried to use the last time I went to the country."

"Very good, my Lord," the butler replied, "There is a note here for your Lordship."

"A note?" Lord Melburne queried, taking the envelope from the silver salver that was held out to him.

Even before he touched it, he knew who it was from. He was scowling as he walked down the hall towards the library where he habitually sat when he was alone.

A footman hurried to open the door for him and he passed into the long book-lined salon which, with its lapis-lazuli pillars and carved gilt cornices, was one of the most beautiful rooms in London.

"Wine, my Lord?" the footman asked.

"I will help myself," Lord Melburne replied.

As the door closed behind the footman, he stood for a moment staring at the note in his hand before he opened it.

He knew only too well who it was from, and he wondered whether this was, in fact, the answer and the solution to the problems that had beset him in the carriage.

Should he get married? Would that state prove more pleasant and at least quieter than the continual lamentations of droxies?

Slowly, it seemed, almost reluctantly, he opened the letter.

Lady Romayne Ramsey's elegant, somewhat affected handwriting was characteristic and yet anyone who had a knowledge of such things would have sensed at once that there was also determination in the fine strokes of her pen.

The note was short.

"My dear Unpredictable Cousin,

I had anticipated that you would call on me this evening, but I was disappointed. I have many things concerning which I desire to speak with you. Come tomorrow at 5 o'clock when we can be alone.

Yours Romayne."

There was nothing particular in the note to annoy his Lordship, yet suddenly he crumpled it in his hands into a tight ball and threw it into the flames of the fire.

He knew in that moment exactly what Romayne Ramsey was after as he had known for a long time that she intended to marry him.

A distant cousin of his, she had presumed on their slight relationship to include him in her intimate circle of friends long before he had made up his mind whether he wished it or not.

And yet it would have been churlish not to be pleased. Lady Romayne was the toast of St. James's, the most beautiful and the most acclaimed 'Incomparable' that the Carlton House Set had known for years.

She had been married when she was but a child, married hastily because her parents had been afraid of her beauty. It was not their fault that Alexander Ramsey, a worthy country Squire, who was excessively wealthy, had broken his neck out hunting just before Romayne's twenty-third birthday.

Long before her mourning had conventionally ended, she had come to London, taken a house, found herself a complaisant chaperone and set St. James's by the ears.

She was lovely, she was vivacious, she was witty and she was rich. What more could any man want of a wife?

And she had chosen Buck Melburne to be her husband.

He was aware of this if no one else was. He was too experienced and too sophisticated in the ways of women not to realise how well planned were her little subterfuges of needing his advice, of asking his opinion, of relying on him as a relative to escort her to Royal functions and to sponsor her as she had no husband to do it for her.

She wove her web about him like a diligent and crafty little spider, but, he told himself, he was not caught yet.

It might indeed be the solution and it might be what he wanted, but he was not sure.

Romayne would look magnificent in the Melburne jewels. She would grace his table and his house in the country with an elegance that was undeniable.

He also realised that there was something dark and passionate in the depth of her eyes when they were alone, that when he kissed her hand goodnight, her breath came more quickly between her parted lips and the laces at her breasts were tumultuous.

He had been so very near to surrendering to her enticement, to the unspoken invitation he saw in her eyes and the way that she would invariably ask him to see her into the darkness of her house when they had been at a party.

There were candles lit in the open door of her bedroom and yet Buck Melburne, for all his reputation as an inveterate lady killer and for never refusing a beautiful woman's favour, had not succumbed to Lady Romayne.

The trap had been too obviously baited. He felt a repugnance against doing exactly what was expected of him, of participating in a campaign that had been planned down to the tiniest detail and of which he knew the inevitable end.

'Damn it, I like to do my own hunting!' he said to himself once as he had come from Lady Romayne's house, well aware of the invitation offered and unexpectedly feeling a cad because he rejected it.

Nothing was ever overtly said and yet they both knew that they faced each other just like duellists. She was taking the offensive, trying to gain an advantage to force him into a corner and he was fighting not for his life but for his freedom.

The flames burned Lady Romayne's letter to ashes and, as it crumpled into nothing, Lord Melburne said again aloud,

"Be damned to all women! A man would be well rid of the lot of them!"

*

When he set off the next morning, tooling his high perch phaeton, the sunshine glittering on the silver bridles of his perfectly matched horseflesh, he was in a surprisingly good mood.

It was a relief, he thought, to be getting out of London. Inevitably one stayed up too late, drank too much and talked a lot of nonsense. Even the duel of wits across the card tables at White's Club or the glittering elegance of the Receptions at Carlton House, lost their interest if one had too much of them.

It was pleasant to know that he was driving the most expensive and the best-bred horses that could be found in anyone's stable, that his new high perch phaeton was lighter and better sprung than the one built for the Prince of Wales.

And he was going to see Melburne again.

There was something about his home that had always delighted him and, while he did not visit it as often as he might wish, it was always a satisfaction to him to know that it was there.

The great house, which had been rebuilt almost entirely by his father to the design of the Adam brothers, stood on the site of older and less spectacular mansions, which had housed generations of Melburnes since the time of the Norman conquest.

As a child, he had loved the gardens, the shrubberies, the lakes, the forest and the great broad acres stretching away over the countryside towards the blue of the Chiltern Hills.

Melburne! Yes, this was the time of year to see Melburne, when the miracle of spring would transform the gardens into a Fairyland of blossom and fragrance.

It was almost irritating to remember that the real object of his coming to the country now was to visit Sir Roderick Vernon. His nearest neighbour and an old friend of his father, Sir Roderick had been very much a part of his childhood.

Hardly a day passed when Sir Roderick with his son Nicholas did not ride or drive over to Melburne or Buck had not accompanied his father to The Priory. The two old gentlemen had argued over their estates, quarrelled over the boundaries and yet remained firm friends until Lord Melburne's father had died at the age of sixty-four.

Sir Roderick had lived on and Lord Melburne, calculating the years as he drove, realised that he must now be nearly seventy-two. He remembered hearing that he had not been well of late and wondered if he was dying.

It was then his conscience smote him for not having gone to The Priory earlier, as he had been asked to do. The letter was clearly urgent and yet it had seemed unimportant beside the attractions of Liane and the many social engagements that he had committed himself to.

He tried to remember the letter now. It had been written by a woman, someone of whom he had never heard. Clarinda Vernon.

Who was she?

Sir Roderick had no daughter and, when he had last visited The Priory there had been no one there except for the old man himself, bewailing the fact that his son Nicholas seldom left London to visit the estates that he would one day inherit.

Nicholas had been a considerable disappointment to his father. He had got into the wrong set in London and indeed Lord Melburne seldom saw him and, if he did, did his best to avoid him.

There were unpleasant stories about Nicholas's behaviour, but Lord Melburne could not remember them now. He only knew that he no longer cared for his childhood friend, in fact, they had hardly spoken to each other since they had left Oxford University.

What had the woman said in her letter?

"My uncle, Sir Roderick Vernon, is ill and greatly desires to see your Lordship. May I beg you to visit him at your earliest convenience.

I remain, my Lord,
Yours Respectfully,
Clarinda Vernon."

This had not told him much except that the old main was ill.

'I should have gone last week,' Lord Melburne said to himself and pushed his horses a little faster, almost as if it was not too late to make up for lost time.

He did not stop at Melburne on the way, as he longed to do, but drove straight to The Priory. It was less than a two hour journey from London and he turned in at the ancient iron gates, noting with satisfaction that despite the speed they had travelled at his horses had stood the journey well and were neither overheated nor in the least fatigued.

The drive was an avenue of ancient oak trees, their branches meeting overhead to make a tunnel of green. As he journeyed on down the drive, Lord Melburne was suddenly aware of someone coming towards him.

It was a woman on a horse and he noted almost automatically that she rode well yet was keeping to the centre of the drive and making no effort to draw aside to let him pass.

Then to his surprise she drew her horse to a stop and waited for his approach, knowing that he must also check his horseflesh and bring them to a standstill.

She sat waiting for him with an imperiousness that definitely irritated him. She did not raise her hand, she just waited and he had an absurd impulse to challenge her by driving over the grass and passing her.

Then, as if in obedience to her unspoken command, he drew in his reins.

Without haste, moving her horse forward, she came to him and stopped by the driving seat. Even so they were not level and she still had to look up at him.

At the first glance he was astonished at her loveliness. He noticed, because he was well versed in women's fashions, that she wore an old habit that was outdated and yet the worn green of its velvet threw into prominence the whiteness of her skin.

Lord Melburne thought he had never seen a woman with such a white skin and then as he looked at her hair he understood. It was red, and yet it was not, it was gold – he was not sure.

It was a colour that he had never seen before or even imagined, the gold of ripened corn flecked with the vivid red of flames leaping from a wood fire. It just seemed to shine in the sunlight and was caught unfashionably into a bun at the nape of her neck. She wore no hat.

She was very small Lord Melburne thought and he realised that while her face was tiny, heart-shaped and with a little pointed chin, her eyes were enormous. Strange eyes for a red-head for they were the very deep blue of a stormy sea rather than hazel flecked with green that might be expected with such colouring.

'She is lovely, unbelievably lovely,' Lord Melburne told himself and then, as he raised his hat, the girl on the horse in a cold voice without smiling, almost demanded,

"You are Lord Melburne?"

"I am."

"I am Clarinda Vernon, I wrote to you."

"I received your letter."

"I expected you last week."

It was an accusation and Lord Melburne felt himself stiffen.

"I regret it was not convenient for me to leave London so speedily," he answered.

"You are still in time."

He raised his eyebrows.

"I must speak with you alone." she asserted.

He glanced at her in surprise feeling they were already alone. Then he remembered the groom behind him on the phaeton.

"Jason," he ordered, "go to the horses' heads."

"Very good, my Lord."

The groom jumped to the ground and went forward to hold the leader of the tandem.

"Shall we speak here," Lord Melburne asked, "or would you rather I come down?"

"This will do," she said, "if your man cannot hear."

"He cannot hear," Lord Melburne replied, "and if he did he is trustworthy."

"What I have to say is not for servants' ears," Clarinda Vernon remarked.

"Perhaps I had best get down," Lord Melburne suggested.

Without waiting for an answer, he sprang lithely to the ground. It was a relief after sitting so long, he thought, to stretch his legs.

"What about your horse?" he asked. "Would you like Jason to hold him too?"

"Kingfisher will not wander away," she answered and then before he could assist her she dismounted with a lightness that seemed as if she almost floated from the saddle.

She slipped the reins over the pommel and turning walked up the drive into the shadows of one of the great oak trees. And Lord Melburne followed her.

She was indeed tiny, even smaller than she had seemed when mounted on her horse. Her waist, even in her worn habit, could easily, he felt, be spanned by a man's two hands and her hair as she moved away from him was like a light will-o'-the-wisp beckoning a man across a treacherous marsh.

He found himself smiling at his own imagination.

'Damn it all, I am getting romantic,' he thought.

He had certainly not expected to find anyone quite so exquisite, so unusual or indeed so beautiful at The Priory.

Clarinda Vernon came to a stop under one of the oaks.

"I had to speak to you before you see my uncle," she said and now Lord Melburne was aware that she was nervous.

"He is ill?" Lord Melburne enquired.

"He is dying," she answered. "I think he has only held on to life so that he should see you."

"I am sorry. If you had been more explicit in your letter, I would have come sooner."

"Indeed I should not have asked your Lordship to forgo your amusements unless it was absolutely necessary."

There was a note of sarcasm in her voice that made him glance at her in surprise.

There was a little pause and then she went on,

"What I have to say will perhaps be difficult for you to – understand. For my uncle's sake it is imperative that you accede to his wishes."

"What does he want?" Lord Melburne asked.

"My uncle." Clarinda replied, "is disinheriting his son Nicholas. He is leaving The Priory and the estate to – me. And because it means so much to him and because he is dying, he has one idea and one idea only in his mind that – no one can change."

"Which is?" Lord Melburne asked as she paused.

"That you should – marry – me!"

Now there was no mistaking the nervous tremor in her voice and the colour rose in her pale cheeks. For a moment Lord Melburne was too surprised to say anything.

Then before even an exclamation could come to his lips Clarinda added quickly,

"All I am asking of you is that you will agree. Uncle Roderick is dying – he may be dead in the morning. Don't argue with him – don't cause him unnecessary distress – just agree to what he asks. It will make him happy and it will mean nothing – nothing to you."

"I really don't think this is something that I can decide on the spur of the moment," Lord Melburne began, for once in his life almost bereft of words.

Then Clarinda Vernon looked up at him with what he could only describe to himself as a violent hatred in her eyes.

"Indeed, my Lord, you need not be afraid that I should hold you to your promise once my uncle is dead for I assure you that I would not marry you – not if you were the last man in the whole world."

There was so much passion in her low voice that it just seemed to vibrate between them.

Then before Lord Melburne could collect his senses and before he could find anything to say and before he even realised what was happening, Clarinda gave a little whistle.

Her horse came obediently to her call and she vaulted unaided into the saddle and was galloping away down the drive towards The Priory as if all the devils of Hell were at her heels.

CHAPTER TWO

Sir Roderick's tired old voice faltered into silence and he fell asleep. His physician bent forward, felt his pulse and said in a low voice to Lord Melburne,

"He will sleep now for some hours."

"I will return later," Lord Melburne replied.

He walked quietly across the bedroom and opened the door. Outside to his astonishment he found a footman bending down, his ear to the keyhole.

When he saw Lord Melburne, he straightened himself up, stared at him for a moment in what seemed an insolent manner and then turned and ran down the corridor as fast as his legs could carry him.

Lord Melburne raised his eyebrows and walked down the staircase. When he reached the hall, he hesitated for a moment and the butler came forward to inform him,

"Miss Clarinda is in the salon, my Lord."

"Thank you," Lord Melburne nodded.

He walked towards the salon, noting as he did so that the house was shabby and badly in need of refurbishing. Some of the high curtains were threadbare and, while the pictures and furniture were extremely valuable, the carpets were worn and many of the chairs in need of upholstery.

Clarinda was sitting at a writing desk in the window.

The sun coming through the open casement shone on her hair and made it appear as if she wore a halo of fire.

At Lord Melburne's entrance she started to her feet and her large dark blue eyes seemed to him to hold not only a hostile but a very wary look. At the same time there was an obvious question in the expression on her face.

"Your uncle has fallen asleep," Lord Melburne told her.

"You have promised what he – asked?"

It seemed as though she could not prevent the question bursting from between her lips.

"We have discussed the matter" Lord Melburne answered.

He felt that she relaxed as if she had been half-afraid that he would refuse outright to do what was requested of him.

Then walking towards the fireplace, he said,

"I understand you are not, in point of fact, Sir Roderick's niece."

"No, my mother was married first to Captain Patrick Wardell of the Grenadier Guards. He was killed fighting before I was born."

She paused for a moment and then, as Lord Melburne said nothing, she continued,

"When my mother married Sir Roderick's brother, he adopted me as his own and had my name changed to Vernon. I thought of him as my father and, as he had no other children, I think he often forgot that I was not in reality his own daughter."

Her voice softened and Lord Melburne noticed that it had a soft musical quality about it.

She had changed from the shabby green habit in which he had first seen her and was now wearing a simple muslin dress, threadbare with washing and unfashionable in shape. And yet he thought, as he had thought before, that she was almost breathtakingly lovely.

There was no need for her strangely alluring hair to be fashionably dressed. It framed the piquancy of her tiny face and he noted that unexpectedly her eyelashes were dark. He thought that perhaps there was some Irish blood in her.

Then sharply, as if she was annoyed at Lord Melburne persuading her into speaking so warmly of her adoptive uncle, Clarinda said in the hard cold voice that she had used to him previously,

"I have something here for your Lordship's approval."

As she spoke, she picked up from the desk a large sheet of paper and held it towards him.

"What is it?" Lord Melburne asked before he had even accepted it from her hand.

"A safeguard against your obvious fear of being trapped into matrimony."

"So you suspicion that I am afraid of that most enviable estate?" he asked her a sudden twinkle in his eye.

"I am not interested in your Lordship's feelings," Clarinda answered coldly. "I can only assure you once again that all that concerns me is that my uncle, who has shown me every possible kindness since I have lived with him, should die happy."

"So Sir Roderick is greatly worried about his estate," Lord Melburne remarked.

"It is all he has thought about, all he cares about and all he loves," Clarinda said almost passionately, "His son has failed him. Can you not understand it will be agony for him to die feeling that his life work will be destroyed or neglected? And he has, I understand, been fond of your Lordship since you were a boy."

She said the words as if it was impossible to credit such affection.

There was a slight twist to Lord Melburne's lips as he glanced down at the paper she had handed him.

On it she had written,

"I, Clarinda Vernon, swear that under no circumstances whatsoever will I hold my Lord Melburne to any promises he might make of Betrothal or Marriage to me once my uncle, Sir Roderick Vernon, is dead. To this I set my hand duly witnessed on Thursday, May 2nd, 1802."

Below was Clarinda's signature and below that again, in illiterate writing, the names of two servants. She saw Lord Melburne glance at them and she said quickly,

"They did not see anything but my signature."

"This is very business-like," Lord Melburne approved, "And now, if in further talks with your uncle I agree to your wishes, I think I should ask the reason why you have such a dislike of me."

Clarinda drew herself up and the colour rose in her cheeks.

"That is something I am not prepared to discuss, my Lord."

"Then I will say," Lord Melburne retorted, "that, as you have made your feelings so very clear, I consider that I am entitled to an explanation."

"I think that is unnecessary – " Clarinda began, but as she spoke, the door opened and a gentleman entered the room.

He was obviously very young but dressed in the height of fashion, the points of his collar high above his chin, his cravat elegantly tied and his hair so beautifully arranged that it must have taken him many laborious hours.

He crossed the room, a jewelled fob dangling from his brocade waistcoat and then raised Clarinda's hand to his lips.

"I have brought you some flowers," he said, offering her the bouquet he held in his hand.

"Orchids!" Clarinda exclaimed. "How very opulent!"

The young man smiled.

"I had to steal them when my father was not looking," he then admitted. "You know how jealously he guards his orchid house."

"Oh, Julien, you should not have taken them," Clarinda cried.

Then, as if she remembered her manners, she turned towards Lord Melburne.

"May I present to you, Mr. Julien Wilsdon, my Lord. Julien, this is Lord Melburne, our next door neighbour, as you well know."

The young man had obviously not seen Lord Melburne as he entered the room, having eyes only for Clarinda. He stared almost incredulously at his Lordship before he exclaimed,

"What is that man doing here? You have always said you would not have him in the house. Has he upset you?"

"No, indeed," Clarinda said rapidly. "I have not had time, Julien, to explain to you Uncle Roderick's wishes where they concern Lord Melburne. He is here for a special purpose and I beg of you to forget what I have said in the past."

"Surely it is impossible for me to do that?" Julien Wilsdon replied.

"Perhaps you would be kind enough to enlighten me as to what this exchange of civilities is about?" Lord Melburne said and there was then a faint twinkle of amusement in his eyes. "Apparently it concerns myself and yet I am very much in the dark as to how I am involved?"

"I only know, my Lord," Julien Wilsdon said abruptly, "that Miss Vernon has very good reasons for not wishing to make the acquaintance of your Lordship."

"Please, Julien, please," Clarinda interrupted. "I can assure you that Lord Melburne is here by invitation. Sir Roderick needed to see him urgently. I will explain everything later. Do, pray, come back this afternoon."

"Perhaps I should inform you, Mr. Wilsdon," Lord Melburne then drawled, "that there is a question as to whether Miss Vernon and I should become betrothed."

He meant what he said to be provocative and he certainly succeeded.

"Betrothed!" Julien Wilsdon almost shouted the word. "It is not true, it really cannot be! How dare you say anything that involves the good name of Miss Vernon? I swear, my Lord, if you are making a mockery of her, I will call you out."

The amusement in Lord Melburne's eyes deepened. Julien Wilsdon was only a thin slip of a youth. His Lordship could not help being aware of the contrast between the young man's immaturity and his own strength, his broad shoulders and above all his height.

As if she too was conscious of the difference between the two men, Clarinda hastily put her arm through Julien Wilsdon's and drew him towards the door.

~25~

"I beg you, Julien, not to make a cake of yourself," she pleaded. "I assure you that what his Lordship is saying has a foundation of fact and I will explain everything. But not now. Wait for me, if you wish, and I will tell you what this is about when his Lordship has left."

Unwillingly and with one backward glance of extreme enmity at Lord Melburne, Julien Wilsdon allowed himself to be led from the salon. He could hear their voices arguing in the hall until finally, after some minutes, Clarinda returned alone.

"I must – apologise," she said in a low voice.

"A very ardent admirer, I see," Lord Melburne commented, "and a dangerous rival."

"Don't try to humiliate me," Clarinda said sharply. "It would not have been correct for me to confide in Julien before you had spoken with my uncle. Now he is enraged and it will be difficult to soothe his hurt feelings."

"I imagine that the whole world cannot be informed that what you contemplate is to be but a pretence," Lord Melburne said. "There would surely be someone to relate to your uncle that he is being hoodwinked."

Clarinda clasped her small hands together anxiously.

"No indeed, you are right about that, my Lord. Until my uncle dies we must make quite sure that no one suspects that our betrothal is just a temporary measure. Once he is dead you need never see me again."

"Surely a somewhat drastic condition," Lord Melburne said. "I am, may I just say, Miss Vernon, finding our acquaintance most enjoyable."

"This may seem a joke to you, my Lord," Clarinda replied crossly, "but I assure you that only the deep affection I have for my uncle and his almost despairing efforts to secure the preservation of his estates would force me to agree to his suggestion."

"And now maybe we can continue with our conversation where it was broken off," Lord Melburne suggested. "Let me put the question very simply, Miss Vernon, why have you such a dislike of me and why indeed is your distaste so virulent that you have discussed it with our other neighbours, such as Mr. Julien Wilsdon?"

He saw the colour rising again in her cheeks and her eyelashes fluttered shyly.

"It was indeed wrong of me to discuss you with anyone else, my Lord, and I must ask your forgiveness. I spoke in confidence and I admit rashly, but it was, I promise you, with no one but Julien, who is the only person I have had to talk for these past months while my uncle has been so ill."

"You are alone here?" Lord Melburne enquired.

"Yes, alone," Clarinda answered. "When I first came here, my uncle had his sister living with him, but she died and there has never been anyone to take her place. Do not think I am complaining – my uncle has been a most interesting companion. I have helped him with the estate, in fact I think I know nearly as much about it as he does. As I suspect he has told you, he has been his own Agent for some years, preferring to deal with the day to day problems himself rather than entrust them to anyone else."

"Why does he care for it so much?" Lord Melburne asked her.

"I think when Nicholas failed him it was all he had left," Clarinda answered quietly. "He loves it. Every penny he has must be spent on improving the farms, draining the fields, trying out new crops and buying new implements. It is his child and his baby, he would give it his life-blood."

She spoke with an almost passionate feeling in her voice and then added rapidly,

"But this is of no interest to your Lordship. The physician has assured me that my uncle cannot linger more than a day or two. Allow him to die happy, then you can return to London and to your own amusements."

"I am grateful for your permission," Lord Melburne said with a touch of sarcasm.

"That is what you want, surely," Clarinda asked. "Your Lordship has little interest in the country, I understand, for you are seldom at Melburne, which is a far larger and finer estate than this."

"I see you know a great deal about my movements," Lord Melburne said suavely. "And now, which of my misdeeds, and I can assure you there are many of them, has thrown you into such a frenzy?"

She heard the sneer in his voice and, looking up into his face, thought how cynical and imperturbable he looked. It could not really matter to him what she thought of him and yet his grey eyes searched her face and were uncomfortably penetrating.

"Well?" he prompted. "Would you like me to make you a full confession of my sins?"

He saw the sudden flash of anger in her eyes. It was almost impossible, he thought, not to provoke her, not to note the changing expressions in her sensitive little face or to see the way that her small chin went up when she was incensed by him.

"Let me make this quite clear, my Lord," she said, turning away from him and walking to the window. "I have no intention of discussing your behaviour now or at any time. I leave that to your conscience. I had no wish for your company, it is only by some quirk of Fate that we are thrust together."

"How unfortunate," he mocked, "that you must be linked in such intimate circumstances with the man you dislike most in the whole world."

Clarinda turned round to face him.

"That is the truth, my Lord, and I am not afraid to admit it. Yet at the same time I am grateful to you for the help you are giving Uncle Roderick."

"A help that I am considering," Lord Melburne corrected her.

He paused for a moment and then he queried,

"I wonder if perhaps I would be wise to make you tell me the truth before I discuss the matter further?"

"I will not speak of it," Clarinda declared obstinately.

Their eyes met and they stared at each other for a few moments. He was very conscious that there was a hatred and something that almost amounted to fear emanating from her.

Then suddenly he laughed.

"Have it your own way then," he capitulated. "It will be amusing to see how long you can withstand my blandishments and perhaps my bullying to make you tell me of your own free will."

As he finished speaking, Lord Melburne swept her a very elegant bow.

"I am leaving now for Melburne," he said. "I have told the physician I will return later in the afternoon, when I understand that your uncle's Attorney will be present. Until then, Miss Vernon, your obedient servant."

Clarinda curtseyed. He opened the door for her, but, before they passed into the hall, he paused and said,

"There is something I have just remembered, something I think I should mention. When I came from your uncle's room, there was a footman listening at the keyhole. I do *not* know whether you wish the staff to learn of everything that is said here in private."

Somewhat to his surprise her face paled and she passed by him into the hall. Hurrying to where the old butler was standing by the doorway, she asked in a low voice,

"Bates, where is Walter?"

The old man hesitated before he replied,

"I was waiting for his Lordship to leave, Miss Clarinda, and then was about to tell you that Walter has gone."

"Gone?" Clarinda expostulated.

"I understand," the butler continued, "that he borrowed a horse from the stables and set off at a great pace."

"Do you think he will have gone to London to Mr. Nicholas?" Clarinda asked, still in a low voice, but Lord Melburne could hear every word she said.

"I'm afraid so, Miss Clarinda."

It seemed to Lord Melburne that Clarinda went even paler than she had been before.

"There is nothing we can do," she muttered beneath her breath, "but I would not have had Mr. Nicholas know of this so soon."

With what was an obvious effort of self-control, she turned towards her guest.

He took her hand in his, and as he did so he realised that she was trembling. There was nothing he could say in front of the butler and, climbing into his high perch phaeton, which was waiting for him, he set off down the drive towards Melburne.

'What a fantastic morning!' he said to himself beneath his breath.

As ever the first sight of his house gave him a thrill of ownership. The great greystone house with its massive pillared front and the beautifully architectured wings too had a truly magnificent setting with its background of dark trees and the lake that mirrored it in the front.

The statues that ornamented the roof were silhouetted against the blue of the sky and, as he drove down the drive, a flight of white pigeons swept across the iridescent windows and gave the whole scene a Fairytale quality that made its owner feel almost poetical.

'If only I could find a woman who was as beautiful as Melburne,' he thought with an unusual sentimentality.

Suddenly before his eyes there appeared a small heart-shaped face framed by golden red hair such as he had never seen before in his whole life.

'Why the hell does she dislike me?' he asked himself.

On entering the Great Hall, with the grace of its Grecian statues enhanced by the soft apple-green walls that the Adam brothers always favoured, Lord Melburne received a noisy welcome from his dogs and his Major Domo uttered a few well-chosen words of welcome.

"I will have luncheon in half an hour," Lord Melburne said, "and send for Major Foster."

"Major Foster is here already, my Lord," the Major Domo replied. "When we learnt from Hawkins of your Lordship's visit, I informed the Major and he felt sure your Lordship would wish to see him."

"Quite right, I do," Lord Melburne said and walked towards the library where he knew that his Agent would be waiting for him.

Major Foster was a man of over fifty who had served and managed the vast Melburne estates, save for a short time when he had been in the Army, since he was a boy. His Army career had looked like being brilliant until he had been wounded and forced into retirement.

He limped very slightly, but his wound did not inconvenience him and he was, as Lord Melburne knew, the most reliable and efficient Agent any landowner could hope to employ.

He held out his hand and Major Foster, taking it, said in all sincerity,

"I am indeed glad to see your Lordship. It is too long since you paid us a visit."

"I was thinking that myself as I came down the drive. And I have never seen the place look better."

"You will be even more pleased, my Lord, when you can see some of the farm reports," Major Foster said enthusiastically.

"I certainly wish to see them," he answered, "but at the moment I have something else to ask you, Foster. What has Nicholas Vernon been doing?"

"You have heard some rumours, my Lord?" Major Foster queried.

"I have just come from Sir Roderick," Lord Melburne replied. "That is indeed the reason for my visit, he is disinheriting his son."

"I am not surprised," Major Foster said. "There has been gossip and scandal and I was meaning to ask your Lordship's advice next time you visited us."

"What is it all about?" Lord Melburne asked, walking across the room to the grog tray, where he poured himself a drink.

"Do you remember the caves on the Vernon estate?" Major Foster asked unexpectedly. "They burrow into the Chilterns and were originally, I do believe, used by the Romans. Down the centuries they have been exploited at various times and, although you may have visited them when you were a boy, they have almost been forgotten until now."

"Yes, of course, I remember them," Lord Melburne said. "Nicholas and I used to explore them with tapers, frightening ourselves in the dark. I remember always being terrified I would never find the way out. What use are they being put to now?"

"I understand," Major Foster said quietly, "that Mr. Vernon has opened a Hell Fire Club in them."

"Good God!" Lord Melburne cried. "You must be joking! Why, Sir Francis Dashwood, who ran his Hell Fire Club at West Wycombe, died eleven years ago and I always understood that before his death such Clubs were forbidden by Law."

"They are indeed," Major Foster said, "which is why Nicholas Vernon has kept his own particular Club secret. I heard rumours of it perhaps a year ago, but I could not credit such nonsense and thought it was just the gossip of the local country folk. The locals talked about much activity in the caves and I learnt that certain volunteers who had been disbanded from the Army and who were badly in need of work were employed there. I thought at first that the roads on the estate required repairs of chalk, but there were other tales."

"What were they?" Lord Melburne asked insistently.

"There was talk of women being brought down here in covered wagons, of coaches with smart painted Coats of Arms passing through the village at night and then turning off down the half-forgotten road towards the caves. There was chatter of masked men, of orgies, most of which I disbelieved. You know how such stories grow in a small village."

Major Foster paused.

"Go on," Lord Melburne prompted him.

"There was a local scandal," he continued. "There is a girl known just as 'Simple Sarah', who was brought up by old Mrs. Huggins. Your Lordship might well remember her as being a foster mother for some half a century."

"I do recall my mother speaking of her," Lord Melburne said. "She disapproved of the woman and half-suspected that some of the children she fostered were neglected and buried surreptitiously in the garden behind her house."

"They may well have been," Major Foster conceded. "But Sarah, who is obviously a love child, grew up. She is called 'Simple' as she is not entirely of a normal intellect, although I would never have thought of her as being a lunatic or anything in that category."

"And she is pretty?" Lord Melburne queried with a twist of his lips.

"Very pretty, which makes it understandable why Mr. Nicholas Vernon was interested in her."

"What happened?" Lord Melburne quizzed him.

"From all I have heard and remember that all I am relating to your Lordship is hearsay," Major Foster replied. "Sarah was taken to the caves. She came back with wild stories of what had occurred there, of gentlemen robed as monks, of women dressed up as nuns, of strange ceremonies, which sounded very like the worst type of the orgies indulged in by Sir Francis Dashwood. So I made some enquiries."

"What did you find out?" Lord Melburne asked.

"I was told, my Lord," he continued, "by someone who knows Nicholas Vernon well that he had always been obsessed by the Hell Fire Caves of West Wycombe. He was, of course, only a schoolboy when Sir Francis had died and they were closed, but when he left Oxford he developed an intense and unnatural curiosity about them and rode over dozens of times to look at the Mausoleum Sir Francis had built on the top of the hill.

"He plagued people round West Wycombe to tell him stories of what had occurred in the caves. They found him a nuisance and tried to send him away, but apparently he had been very persistent."

"So you think he is following Sir Francis's example?" Lord Melburne said reflectively.

"I'm afraid so, my Lord," Major Foster replied.

"And the villagers are annoyed at Simple Sarah being involved in such unpleasantness," Lord Melburne remarked.

"It was not so much that she was involved, but recently when her baby disappeared the scandal really broke."

"Her baby?" Lord Melburne asked sharply.

"She swore that her child had been fathered by him, Mr. Nicholas Vernon," Major Foster explained. "But a month after it was born it vanished and Sarah was distraught. She had been fond of the child in her own not very intelligent way and she had been, I understand, quite a good mother. When she had lost the baby, she tore about like a demented creature accusing Nicholas Vernon of having sacrificed it in the caves."

"Good God!" Lord Melburne exclaimed.

"There was such an uproar that some of the more responsible of the villagers, headed by the Vicar, went to Sir Roderick. It was obvious, they told me afterwards, that Sir Roderick was not entirely surprised at what they told him about the caves. But, where the child was concerned, he was shocked and horrified.

"From all reports he wrote to his son, Nicholas, telling him that he had disinherited him and that he was never to come to The Priory again."

"So that is what happened. Damme, Foster! I can hardly believe that such things could happen in this day and age."

"In my opinion, Mr. Nicholas Vernon was always a bad young man. I must admit it, my Lord, I never had a liking for him. But I did not think he would sink to such depravity as this."

"And are the caves now closed?" Lord Melburne asked.

"We don't know," Major Foster said. "No one has liked to trespass on Sir Roderick's estate to ascertain if the place is dismantled. I only understand that Mr. Nicholas Vernon has not been here for the last month or so. Anyway, if he has, I have not learnt of it."

There was a pause and then Major Foster asked,

"But you have seen Sir Roderick, my Lord. Did he speak to you of this?"

"Not in so many words," Lord Melburne replied. "But I will be seeing him again this afternoon."

Having no desire to confide to his Agent what Sir Roderick had communicated to him, he then went on to speak of matters connected with his estate. And, as there was a great deal to discuss, luncheon was delayed and it was later than he had calculated before he drove back to The Priory.

Bates, the butler, opened the door to him and, as he took his hat and gloves, he said,

"Miss Clarinda is in the study, my Lord. For the moment she is engaged."

As Lord Melburne turned towards the stairs to go up to Sir Roderick's room, he heard a coarse common voice raised in anger coming from the study on the other side of the hall. It was a man's voice and, seeing the old butler glance uncertainly at the closed door, he asked,

"Who is with Miss Clarinda?"

"One of the farmers, my Lord, a rough man and somewhat violent in his manner."

Lord Melburne crossed the hall and opened the study door. As he did so, he heard a man saying,

"You'll give me the money now or I be goin' upstairs to demand it from Sir Roderick. I knows my rights and you'll give it to me or it'll be the worse for you."

Lord Melburne advanced.

Clarinda was sitting at a large desk in the centre of the room. It was a man's desk and it made her look very small and fragile.

Standing on the other side of it was a big burly man, dark haired and swarthy of skin, who was speaking with an accent that Lord Melburne recognised as being more likely to have come from Billingsgate than from the countryside.

"Can I perhaps be of assistance?" he then asked.

The man, who had his back to the door, turned quickly. His expression was aggressive and almost ferocious, but when he could see Lord Melburne, his expression changed and in an instant he became subservient.

"I were just askin' for me just dues, sir," he said surlily.

"They are not just, as you well know," Clarinda retorted. "You had thirty pounds from the estate three weeks ago for repairs and, when I visited you last week, I could see no sign of them."

"I 'ad to get the materials first, 'adn't I?" the man countered rudely.

"I saw no sign of those either," Clarinda answered him.

"I'll be a talkin' with Sir Roderick about the monies," the man carried on.

It was quite obvious to Lord Melburne that it was a threat rather than any desire to see the owner of the estate.

"As Sir Roderick is not well," Lord Melburne said, "I will send my Agent, Major Foster, over to your farm tomorrow. He will advise Miss Vernon as to whether or not you are entitled to any more payment."

"I be entitled to it right enough," the man persisted. "Mr. Nicholas knows 'ow much I be entitled to."

"Then I would suggest that you go and ask Mr. Nicholas Vernon for your requirements," Lord Melburne said and his voice was like a whip, "for I have a suspicion that you are neither a good farmer nor even a genuine one. Indeed I should not be surprised if the Bow Street Runners would not be interested in your whereabouts in this part of the country."

Even as he spoke a complete transformation came over the man.

For one moment he looked as though he would defy Lord Melburne, then his defiance crumbled and, with a shifty surreptitious look towards the door, he said,

"I gets your meanin', sir. No need to send anyone to the farm, I be a-clearin' out."

"I thought so," Lord Melburne replied, "and the sooner the better. My Agent will come tomorrow to see if you have kept your word and departed."

It was doubtful if the man heard the last part of Lord Melburne's sentence. Already he was through the door, closing it sharply and they heard his footsteps hurrying across the hall.

Lord Melburne looked at Clarinda and saw that, although she held herself proudly, there was a touch of fear in her eyes.

"How did you know," she asked, "that he was not what he seemed?"

"It was quite obvious that he was not a countryman," Lord Melburne pointed out.

"Nicholas sent him here just two months ago," she explained, "and I did not dare worry Uncle Roderick because he was so ill. I let him have the farm though I knew it was a mistake. He has been forcing me to give him money ever since."

"Which farm is it?" Lord Melburne asked.

"The one at Coombe's Bottom," she answered.

He nodded.

"I know it. I will tell Foster to find you a decent tenant."

"I don't wish to put your Lordship to any unnecessary trouble," Clarinda said in a low voice.

"Are there any more of Nicholas's *protégés* on the estate at the moment?" he asked.

She hesitated a moment.

"You had much better tell me," he suggested in a kind voice.

"There is only one," she answered, "except for Walter, the footman, whom you saw this morning. Nicholas insisted on our employing him."

"And the other?"

"A man who came here ten days ago. He wanted Dene's Farm near the caves."

As she spoke the words, the colour rose in her cheeks and Lord Melburne knew that she had heard about the caves.

"Who is this man?" he asked.

"He is very strange. He looks more like a Priest than a farmer. He had two men with him, I don't know whether they were relations. Anyway Nicholas wrote me most insistently that he was to be given the farm. Someone must have told him that it was vacant."

"And you gave it to him?" Lord Melburne enquired.

"What else could I do?" she asked. "I could not discuss new tenants with Uncle Roderick in his present state of health and I have no authority to refuse Nicholas. The man moved in, I understand, three days ago."

"You did not like him?"

"There was something horrible about him," she answered with a little shudder. "I cannot quite explain, but he frightened me."

"I will tell Foster to look at that farm as well," Lord Melburne proposed.

"I don't want to trespass on your Lordship's kindness," Clarinda said, "but there does not seem for the moment anything else I can do."

"I see it goes against the grain for you to accept any favours from me. Shall I promise you that I will not take advantage of your weakness?"

For a moment she raised her chin almost as though he had insulted her and then she said,

"I suppose you are right, my Lord, it is weakness. It is when you are up against people like that man you have just seen and also the one who has moved into Denes Farm, that one realises how hopeless it is to be a woman."

"And you would prefer to be a man?" Lord Melburne asked, thinking how exquisitely feminine she looked with her big troubled eyes, a little droop at the corner of her lips and the much-washed white muslin revealing the soft curves of her breasts.

"I hate it, if you want to know!" she replied with a sudden rush of spirit. "I wish I was a man, a man who could fight and control such creatures as those, a man who did not have to coax, intrigue and beg for favours because he is too frail to demand them."

Lord Melburne gave a cynical laugh.

"As you grow a little older, you will find it, I assure you, far easier to get what you want by being a beautiful woman rather than a brawny man."

He spoke almost caressingly, simply because he was bemused by her loveliness.

She looked up at him in surprise and for a moment he held her eyes.

Then sharply she turned away and said in her most icy tone,

"As far as you are concerned, my Lord, I would most certainly wish to be a man."

CHAPTER THREE

Lord Melburne awoke with a feeling of pleasurable anticipation that he had not felt since he was a boy.

For a moment he wondered where he was and then, seeing the carved posts of his huge bed silhouetted against the faint light peeping in through the sides of the curtains, he realised that he was still at Melburne.

He was conscious at the same time of a feeling of wellbeing and recognised that it was quite a long time since he had woken with such a clear head.

He had gone to bed early and, although he had expected to lie awake, he had slept almost as soon as his head touched the pillow.

His second day at home, although he had not expected it, had been extremely busy.

The wind coming through the open casement window blew the curtains apart and for a brief second a golden shaft of sunshine entered the room. It reminded him of Clarinda's hair and he found himself thinking about her.

Lord Melburne was not a particularly conceited man, but he would have been a fool if he had not realised that, when a woman of any age looked at him, her face softened and her eyes appreciated his good looks.

He would have been half-witted if he had not known that he had only to pay a woman a compliment or look at her admiringly for a gleam of excitement to show in her eye and that, when he kissed her hand, if his lips lingered on her soft skin, her breath came a little quicker between her parted lips.

And yet this country wench, this unsophisticated chit, who apparently had seen nothing at all of the world, could look at him with undisguised hatred and her voice when she spoke to him could be colder than the wind blowing from Siberia.

Why did she hate him?

What was the secret behind her hostility?

Lord Melburne was forced to admit that he was intrigued. He had expected to post back to London today bored with the country, eager for the companionship of his friends and the gaiety of the Clubs, the parties and the gaming halls they frequented so often.

But he knew now that he had no intention of leaving Melburne until he found the answer to a number of questions that puzzled him.

It was not only Clarinda who intrigued him.

Yesterday afternoon, after he had spent time with Sir Roderick, he and Major Foster had ridden out to look at the caves. It was many years since Lord Melburne had been that way and he noticed at once that the lane had been repaired and widened.

At one time it had been almost impossible to get even a horse with any ease between the trees and shrubs sloping down from the Chiltern Hills to the very edge of the farmed fields with their sprouting wheat.

But now what had been a track had become a road wide enough to allow the passage of a coach and four and, when they reached the caves themselves, it was to find that a large gravel sweep had been laid down outside the entrance and then the entrance itself had certainly been transformed.

Lord Melburne had looked at Major Foster.

"This has cost money," he commented.

"It is exactly in the Dashwood tradition," Major Foster murmured.

They both stared at the great wrought-iron gateway, at the moment securely held by a padlock. There were sconces on either side ready to hold flaring torches and there were yew trees, some obviously transplanted, some in large tubs and a general air of sophistication very different from the bramble-covered wilderness that Lord Melburne remembered as a boy.

A little further on they found a huge stack of chalk that had clearly been excavated from the caves themselves and a place where carriages could wait.

Then, as there seemed little more to see, they rode towards the small farmhouse only two hundred yards from the entrance to the caves and standing in the middle of lush green fields.

"Burrows, who farmed this land for forty years, died last month," Major Foster said. "I understood that the place was empty."

"Miss Vernon told me that it had been occupied in the last three days," Lord Melburne said. "Nicholas Vernon sent down someone from London."

"Another of his riff-raff!" Major Foster exclaimed. "You were right, my Lord, about the other man. When I visited the farm yesterday, he had cleared out. There was no one there."

"I thought he would," Lord Melburne said. "I suspicioned as soon as I looked at him that he was the type that would be wanted by the Bow Street Runners."

"Heaven knows where Nicholas Vernon finds these people," Major Foster muttered.

As they reached the farm, they drew in their horses for coming from the door towards them was a strange-looking man wearing an old and rather dilapidated cassock.

Lord Melburne saw at once why Clarinda had thought that he looked more like a Priest than a farmer. He was fat and his shaven face had an expression of one who is used to good living. His head was bare and what little hair he had was turning grey.

There was something in the expression on his face and in his narrow dark-circled eyes that struck Lord Melburne as being particularly unpleasant.

"What do you want?" the man asked in an educated voice.

"I am Lord Melburne, your near neighbour," Lord Melburne replied, "and this is Major Foster, my Agent. I understand you are a newcomer here."

"Have you any jurisdiction over this land?" the stranger in the cassock asked.

"No," Lord Melburne replied, "we were just calling on you out of courtesy."

"That is unnecessary," he replied, "so I will bid you good day, gentlemen. I have no time to waste on callers."

He turned as he spoke and walked back to the door of the farmhouse. The door closed behind him and Lord Melburne looked at Major Foster.

"Charming manners," he said sarcastically, "and what the devil is he doing here?"

"I imagine that only Mr. Nicholas Vernon could supply the answer to that question."

Lord Melburne glanced towards the caves.

"I dislike my own suspicions about him," he said almost to himself.

They rode back towards the main highway.

"I wonder what I ought to do about all this?" Lord Melburne mused. "You might say it is none of my business, but with Sir Roderick so ill, Nicholas Vernon disinherited and that girl to all intents and purposes alone at The Priory, I feel I have a certain responsibility."

"I think you have a very great responsibility, my Lord, if you will forgive my saying so," Major Foster said. "You are of vast import in the County. I don't think you can allow such scandals to continue unchecked."

"I see what you mean," Lord Melburne replied. "At the same time I have no desire to make allegations without being able to prove them. From all you tell me we have only the word of a village maiden, noted for being to let in the attic, that she has taken part in some sort of orgy and that she suspects the son of one of our most reputable landowners of having abducted her baby. Now you know as well as I do, Foster, that that sort of rumour would not hold water in any Court of Law."

Major Foster sighed.

"No, indeed, my Lord, we will have to do better than that."

"*You* will have to do better, you mean," Lord Melburne said insistently. "Find out more, Foster, discover when Nicholas Vernon is holding his next party in the caves. If I am not very much mistaken, the person who could tell us that quite accurately is that seedy-looking Cleric we have just left at Dene's Farm."

"Why in Heaven's name should Nicholas Vernon require a Parson?"

Lord Melburne looked at his Agent and made as if to answer his question and then he changed his mind.

"I am convinced," he continued, speaking seriously, "that mere speculations on what has occurred are a mistake. We need facts, Foster, facts and proof that something untoward is taking place here."

He brought his hand down hard on his saddle.

"Then I promise that I will go to the Lord Lieutenant, I will invoke the Law. I will bring in the Military if necessary. But I must then be absolutely sure before I make any accusations against Vernon or I could make myself a laughing stock."

Lord Melburne had spoken positively and behaved, as he thought, with discretion. At the same time he knew that he was intensely curious.

The rest of the day was fully occupied by his Head Groom, who had several yearlings to show him and was most insistent that he should inspect some horses from a nearby stable that were up for sale.

Lord Melburne, after three hours of hard bargaining, obtained what he thought would prove to be three excellent hunters and returned home in a high good humour.

This morning, as he dressed with the assistance of his valet, he thought that perhaps Major Foster might have more information for him about the caves and, as he went down to breakfast, he admitted to himself that the situation at The Priory interested him far more than anything else had for a long time.

"Nice morning, Newman," he said to his butler as he helped himself to a dish of veal cutlets cooked with cream and fresh mushrooms.

"It's good to see your Lordship in such excellent health," Newman replied.

He was an elderly man who had faithfully served Lord Melburne's father.

"I must come to the country more often," Lord Melburne said, "it obviously agrees with me."

"We shall be more than glad to welcome you, my Lord," Newman answered and Lord Melburne knew that he was speaking the truth.

Having partaken of several dishes and sent his compliments to the cook, Lord Melburne went to the front door where his horse was waiting.

It was a black stallion with a touch of white in his two front fetlocks, a magnificent beast with Arab blood in him, which Lord Melburne had bought at Tattersalls six months ago, sent down to the country and had half-forgotten its very existence.

Now he looked at it appreciatively and realised with a feeling of acute pleasure that he was going to have some difficulty in holding the animal.

The horse was rearing up and it required two grooms to keep it under control until Lord Melburne was in the saddle.

"Saladin be over-fresh, my Lord," one of the grooms remarked unnecessarily, as bucking and rearing the stallion pranced about the drive, doing its best to exert its supremacy over the man it sensed instinctively would eventually master him.

Lord Melburne took Saladin through the Park, checking him from a full gallop for fear of rabbit holes and made his way towards Dingle's Ride, which was the traditional place on his estate to try out fresh horses.

Dingle's Ride lay between the Melburne Estate and Sir Roderick's. It consisted of a large wood and five hundred acres of land that were not worth cultivating. But through the centre of it ran a wide grassy ride that had been the delight of both families since the beginning of time.

Yet they fought over the ownership. On some of the ancient maps Dingle's Ride was shown belonging to Melburne and on others to The Priory.

The ownership had been a lasting bone of contention ever since Lord Melburne could remember and now, with a little smile of triumph on his lips, he recalled that yesterday Sir Roderick had offered Dingle's Ride to him as a present.

He could, of course, have challenged Sir Roderick and said that he already considered Dingle's Ride as part of his own property. But he well knew that he had no real authority for saying so any more than Sir Roderick could actually claim complete ownership himself.

The gift, Lord Melburne knew, was almost in the nature of a bribe. Equally he was very pleased to accept it, knowing it would allay for ever the arguments as to who was the rightful owner.

Saladin was pulling at the bit and doing his best to break into a headlong gallop. It would be interesting, Lord Melburne thought as he made his way through the trees to see how this new purchase could perform when he really gave him his head.

Then, as he came to the Ride, he saw that he was not alone. A little further up, emerging from the other direction, was a figure in a green habit. It was clear that Clarinda saw him at the same time he saw her and, although he was too far away to see the expression on her face, he was sure that her lips tightened and her eyes darkened at the sight of him.

It seemed to the man watching her that she almost instinctively turned as if to avoid him, for touching her horse with her whip, she then set off at a headlong gallop down the Ride, obviously doing her utmost to increase her horse's pace and, thought Lord Melburne with a glint in his eyes, determined to escape him.

She moved so quickly that she had a considerable start on him before Lord Melburne, settling his top hat a little firmer on his head, set out to catch her up.

It was very exhilarating to feel the cool morning breeze on his face, to hear the sound of pounding hoofs and know the excitement of a chase in which he was determined to be the victor.

Clarinda's horse was of good strain, Sir Roderick would never have had poor horseflesh in his stables, but it had not the strength of Saladin with his Arab blood. Even so Clarinda had a long start on him and, what was more, he thought, watching her ahead, she rode superbly.

She was not wearing a hat and her hair, glinting in the early sunshine, had merely been plaited and caught up into her neck with a bow of green ribbon. It seemed to wave ahead of him almost like a flag enticing him to follow.

Determinedly he urged Saladin forward with a resolution that made him feel that he was riding a race in which the high stakes presented an irresistible lure.

He did not catch up with Clarinda until they had traversed nearly three-quarters of the Ride and then as he drew level he glanced at her and saw that her eyes were shining despite the fact that she was tense. And he was sure that she was willing herself to beat him.

For a little while they galloped on side by side, Clarinda striving, it seemed, with every nerve in her body to draw ahead of him again. Then that realising it was impossible because the end of the Ride was not far ahead, she began to draw in her reins.

Lord Melburne did the same and finally they came to a standstill at the end of Dingle's Ride. They were both breathing quickly and there was a patch of bright colour in Clarinda's cheeks.

With an almost theatrical gesture Lord Melburne swept his hat from his head.

"As an Amazon, I salute you!" he exclaimed.

Thrilled with the excitement of the ride, she then smiled at him unaffectedly, her eyes seeming to reflect the sunshine.

And next provocatively she was challenging him,

"You realise you are trespassing, my Lord."

"On the contrary," he replied, "*you* are the trespasser."

"This land has belonged to The Priory since the reign of Henry VIII," she retorted.

"That is your claim, although I do not admit it," he replied. "But as a matter of fact from tomorrow it will be mine indisputably."

She glanced at him quickly.

"Uncle Roderick has given it to you?" she asked and added almost disdainfully, "A most generous payment surely for such small services as you have been able to render him."

"You are trying to provoke me," Lord Melburne said in an amused voice. "Stop being a little tiger cat and let me compliment you, Miss Vernon, on the way you ride. I have seldom seen a female with a better seat."

Just for a moment he knew that she was pleased by his words. Then, as if the barrier that she had erected between them fell once more into place, she replied coldly,

"I have no need of your approval, my Lord. I understand that you will be calling on my uncle this afternoon. He is looking forward to your visit."

She had moved away almost before she had finished speaking and, riding over the grass, disappeared between the trees in the direction of The Priory.

Lord Melburne sat for a moment on his horse looking after her, a smile on his lips.

And yet it was still irritating as he rode back to Melburne to wonder, as he had already wondered a hundred times, what exactly she had against him.

It was impossible for her, living the quiet life that she had lived here at The Priory, to have come in contact with any of the ladies of Society whose favours he had enjoyed.

What was more, he could not imagine that any of them, considering the high position they graced, would be likely to confide in a country girl, who as far as he could ascertain had never left the peace and security that surrounded The Priory.

He had learnt from Sir Roderick that Clarinda was just nineteen. She had been at The Priory for four years. During that time he was almost certain that she had taken little part in any social life, even in the County, let alone the fashionable Society to be found in London.

Lord Melburne had also learnt something else in his talk with Sir Roderick. Like many elderly people. Sir Roderick had become obsessed with money. He was a rich man, but he could not bear to spend anything except on his beloved estate.

That accounted, of course, for the threadbare condition of the furnishings in the house and the fact that Clarinda was quite obviously in need of a new wardrobe.

Lord Melburne, who had more understanding of human nature than he gave himself credit for, knew that elderly people usually ended up either crazily over-generous or cheese-paring with every penny.

Sir Roderick belonged to the second category with the result that, if indeed he finally left everything to Clarinda, as he intended to do, she would, although doubtless penniless at the moment, be a very considerable heiress.

There were, Lord Melburne thought soberly, a great many problems to be solved. While he pandered to Sir Roderick's obsession that the two estates should be joined in one and that a Melburne should marry a Vernon, he was well aware that the old man's desire to provide for Clarinda took very second place to his anxiety about his lands.

He could not bear to think of the estate not being kept in good condition or not being cared for as he cared for it with his whole heart. He would fight for the Priory Estate with his dying breath and Clarinda was only subsidiary to his main objective.

'I wonder what will become of her?' Lord Melburne asked himself and then shrugged his shoulders.

When Sir Roderick died, it would no longer be any of his business and she certainly would not turn to him for advice. Equally he could not help feeling that Nicholas Vernon was not going to take this in good part.

In other circumstances the sensible course would be for him to be married to his father's adopted niece. There was no blood relationship between them. Yet from all Lord Melburne had learnt of Nicholas's activities, he would not wish him as a husband for any woman, least of all the exquisite unsophisticated Clarinda.

As he rode back through the Park, he found himself thinking how lovely Clarinda would look if she was dressed in the height of fashion. He was ready to wager that there was not an 'Incomparable' in the whole of St. James's who could hold a candle to her.

Even the acclaimed beauty of Lady Romayne would seem hard and even coarse beside the fragility of that small pointed face and the translucence of that clear white skin.

"Lovely and a great heiress!" Lord Melburne said aloud and wondered once again what the devil would happen to her in the future.

Major Foster was waiting at the house with a sheaf of farming statistics.

Lord Melburne put them aside.

"Any more news?" he asked and they both knew what he was referring too.

"I went to call on the Vicar last night," Major Foster replied. "He told me that Simple Sarah is so distraught at the loss of her child that there is talk of her having to be restrained in an asylum."

"Wretched creature," Lord Melburne expostulated. "At the same time I can hardly credit that Nicholas, who after all was born a gentleman, could really sink to such a deed of horror."

"I cannot help feeling that myself," Major Foster agreed. "I also made some enquiries, my Lord, about that odd man we talked to at Dene's Farm. The Vicar tells me he has reason to believe that his name is 'Thornton' and that he is in fact a Parson."

"Why does the Vicar think that?" Lord Melburne asked.

"Apparently there was some scandal three years ago at a Parish near Beaconsfield. The villagers rose in protest and the Parish Priest disappeared. The Vicar, who is quite astute, says the tenant at Dene's Farm does bear a distinct resemblance to the description of the banished Cleric."

"That is another thing we must prove," Lord Melburne said. "The Vicar is guessing. It may be an accurate guess, but it is not evidence, as you well know, Foster."

"No, my Lord, and I shall continue to make further enquiries."

"I hope you will," Lord Melburne answered.

There were many other subjects to speak about and Lord Melburne was quite surprised when luncheon was announced.

After he had eaten well, finding the food surprisingly good when he had thought that his French chef in London would have spoilt him for any other cooking, he went up the stairs to change his clothes.

His phaeton was waiting and he drove towards The Priory in a pleasant state of amused anticipation and an inner satisfaction that might have had something to do with the excellence of the claret that he had consumed at luncheon.

He did not hurry his horses, finding the sunshine pleasant and looking around him at the growing crops. He thought that the woods on the Priory Estate would make excellent cover for nesting pheasants and wondered what the partridge shooting would be like in the autumn.

There would also be partridge shooting at Melburne and he was wondering whether the Prince of Wales would like to be his guest as he drew up briskly outside The Priory.

As he did so, he heard the sound of horses' hoofs behind him and, turning his head in surprise, saw an elegant coach tooled by a smartly liveried coachman coming down the drive behind him.

He thought he recognised the livery, but was convinced that he must be mistaken until, as the coach drew level with him, a lovely familiar face appeared at the lowered window.

"Good afternoon, Buck," Lady Romayne exclaimed and waited for her footman to open the carriage door.

Lord Melburne, in a state of near stupefaction, threw the reins to his groom and jumped down from the high phaeton in time to assist her Ladyship to alight.

"My dear Romayne," he said, raising her fingers to his lips, "what in the name of Jupiter are you doing here?"

"I thought you would be surprised to see me," she answered. "But did you really think that I was not curious to hear what was afoot?"

"Curious about what?" he enquired.

"Now really, Buck, that is doing it too brown!" she replied with a little flirtatious glance over her shoulder as she walked towards the front door. "I arrived at Melburne just after you had left and I then recalled that Sir Roderick Vernon was an old beau of my Mama's. I visited here once many years ago when I was a child. I am certain he will not have forgotten me."

"Sir Roderick is very ill, in fact he is dying," Lord Melburne said. "But you have not yet explained to me, Romayne, why you should post down from London in this unexpected and impetuous manner."

She looked at him and her eyes narrowed for a moment.

"Did you really expect me to do anything else," she asked and her voice was hard, "with Nicholas Vernon proclaiming far and wide that you have become affianced to some unknown female called 'Clarinda'?"

Lord Melburne was silent. He was remembering the listening footman who had set off immediately towards London after his first visit to Sir Roderick. Of course Clarinda had been right. The man had gone in search of Nicholas and related to him all that he had overheard. Now Nicholas Vernon, as he had always anticipated, intended to make trouble.

But what could he say to Lady Romayne?

"I do think, dear Buck, that you might have told me," she was saying wistfully in a soft seductive voice.

He knew her too well not to know that she was seething with anger beneath the apparent gentleness of her words.

"Now listen, Romayne," he said. "As I have already said, Sir Roderick is on the point of death. Go back to Melburne and wait for me there. I will join you in a short time and try to give you a reasonable explanation."

Even as he said the words, Lord Melburne thought with a rising anger that he was going to be hard put to find any explanation let alone a reasonable one.

When he had been forced by Clarinda into this intolerable position, he had not for one moment imagined that the pretended betrothal would be known outside the immediate parties concerned or indeed beyond the gates of The Priory.

With Nicholas babbling about it in London, with Lady Romayne posting to Melburne to make trouble and to find himself at the moment without any explanation for his behaviour was to make Lord Melburne feel a surge of fury towards the author of this nonsensical tangle.

It was all Clarinda's fault, *damn* her! If she had wanted him to enact the Cheltenham Dramatics, she should have arranged things better.

There should not have been a footman listening outside the door and Nicholas Vernon behaving in what he had to admit was a quite predictable manner.

"Wait for me at Melburne," he said to Lady Romayne and it was a command that he knew almost as he said it that she had no intention of obeying.

"I must see this young woman who is to be my new relative," she said. "Why, dear Buck, must you be so secretive? After all you are my cousin. And Miss Clarinda Vernon, whoever she may be, will therefore be a cousin by marriage. Besides I am extremely interested to see her and find out how she has managed to capture your interest so quickly."

Lady Romayne was no fool, as Lord Melburne knew. She was not going to be deceived into thinking that this was a case of love at first sight.

She was well aware that there must be some reason behind the tale that he was betrothed and God knows what Nicholas Vernon may have said.

There was nothing else he could do so he said in an ungracious voice,

"Very well, if that be your wish, come and meet Miss Vernon, although I can assure you, Romayne, there is no reason for you to meddle in my affairs at this stage."

"So have I ever meddled?" she asked softly. "All I have ever desired, my most beloved cousin, has been your happiness."

The fact that she assumed that his happiness still lay with her remained unspoken, but the intention was very obvious as she laid one white hand upon his arm and turned her beautiful face up to his.

Dressed in the height of fashion, her high-crowned bonnet covered with nodding plumes, with the latest Empireline dress beneath her pelisse showing off the curves of her exquisite figure, it was hard to imagine that anyone could be more enticing.

And yet Lord Melburne's eyes were hard as he led the way into the salon.

The room was empty and Lord Melburne, followed by Lady Romayne, walked across the room and out of the French windows onto the terrace, where there was a pervading scent of roses and honeysuckle and the sunshine was warm on their faces.

With a sudden feeling of utter amazement Lord Melburne saw Clarinda standing in the centre of the Rose Garden.

She was not alone. Julien Wilsdon was with her and he had his arms round her, holding her closely against him, his head bent towards hers.

For a moment Lord Melburne stood completely motionless as Lady Romayne gave an amused laugh.

"Poor Buck!" she said, "it appears that already, so soon after your betrothal, you must look to your laurels."

At the sound of her voice, Julien Wilsdon and Clarinda started apart guiltily.

Then, as Julien Wilsdon stared at Lord Melburne, Clarinda, with a little cry like that of a frightened child, turned round and ran from the Rose Garden over the lawn and disappeared behind a clump of lilac bushes.

Just for a moment Lord Melburne hesitated, until without a word to Lady Romayne he turned and walked swiftly after Clarinda.

He had no idea where she had gone, but, as he rounded the lilac bushes behind which she had disappeared, he found a path and, moving along it, his chin set square, his mouth in a hard line, he found her standing outside a rose-covered arbour, in front of which was a small weather-beaten sundial.

He walked up to her and saw that she was still breathing quickly from the speed she had run at. He looked down at her and before she could speak he put out his hands and gripped her by the shoulders.

"How dare you!" he stormed and there was no doubt that he was extremely angry. "How dare you make a fool of me! You ask me to take part in some hair-brained scheme to help your poor uncle and then you insult me by flaunting your lover not only in front of me but in front of my friends."

He was so angry that he shook her and the violence of his action tumbled the red-gold curls around her cheeks.

"You have been rude enough to me by all counts," he said. "I imagined that there was some moral reason for your dislike of me, but now from your own behaviour I doubt it."

He shook her again and as he did so, angry though he was, he realised how incredibly lovely she was with her eyes looking up at him in surprise, her lips parted and a flush in her pale cheeks.

Then brutally, because he was so incensed, he swept her into his arms.

"If it is kisses you want," he asserted harshly, "take them from the man who is entitled to give them to you."

His lips were on hers before she could cry out a word and because of his anger he kissed her roughly and almost cruelly. Suddenly he was aware of the softness and sweetness of her lips beneath his and his mouth became gentler but more possessive.

His anger faded and he felt an irrepressible desire to awaken her and make her respond to him as every woman he had ever kissed in the past had responded.

His kisses were very experienced, very demanding and very persuasive.

Then incredulously Lord Melburne realised that after only one violent effort to struggle against him that had been ineffective, Clarinda was still and passive in his arms.

She was so still that he raised his head in surprise. At once with a quick twist of her body she was free of him. Just for a moment she looked at him, her eyes dark with anger, before she said slowly and coldly,

"I am afraid, my Lord, that your licentious attempts at love-making are not appreciated in the country, however successful they may be in London. If indeed you are hard-pressed to find a woman, there may be a nit witted village maiden who will not refuse your advances."

She spoke without hesitation and it was quite obvious that her speech had been prepared. Then the blood flooded into her cheeks, her eyes flashed fire and she stamped her foot.

"If only I was a man," she cried and spat the words at him, "I would kill you for this!"

She ran away before he could reply, twisting in and out of the shrubs until within a few seconds he could no longer see her.

Lord Melburne stood for some time looking at the place she had vanished from, with a strange expression on his face.

His anger had gone and now he could only think of Clarinda's stillness in his arms, the softness of her lips and then realised incredulously that he had evoked no response in her but hatred.

Never in his whole life had a woman, after he had kissed her, turned from him in dislike and never had the passionate demands of his lips been rejected.

Now he was uncomfortably aware of the ignominious position that his impetuous action had placed him.

He had not meant to insult Clarinda and he had never in his wildest moments intended to force his attentions upon her. But she made him so damned angry, behaving in such a manner in front of Romayne who, with her sharp tongue and her perceptive little brain, would make the very most of such a situation.

Then he knew that, if he was to be honest with himself, it was not only his anger that had made him kiss Clarinda. There had been something irresistibly inviting in her parted lips and the loveliness of her face turned up to his, in the sun shining on her shaken curls and in the incredible whiteness of her skin and her cheeks flushed by his violence.

There was no doubt that by his behaviour he had put himself in the wrong.

She would hate him more than ever now and God knows he deserved it.

"*Your licentious lovemaking*".

What a phrase! He could imagine her thinking it out before she had met him and after she had begun to hate him because of something she had learnt regarding his past. Now she had even more good reason for her dislike.

He was aware that she had meant to remain cool and icy beneath his lips and to freeze him by her very inaction. Yet her anger had swept away her effort at play-acting and he knew that she had looked almost lovelier when she had raged at him than when he had taken her into his arms.

The whole situation was, however, a complicated coil from which he could see no easy escape. Besides Romayne was waiting for him and God knows what he could tell her that would not make the situation worse.

Lord Melburne was frowning as he began to retrace his steps towards the Rose Garden. There was no one to be seen now on the terrace and, as he entered the salon, it was to find Julien Wilsdon waiting for him.

When Lord Melburne appeared, he squared up his shoulders and faced him courageously but he was obviously nervous.

"I have to apologise, my Lord," he said in a low voice.

Lord Melburne merely raised his eyebrows.

"I would not wish you to think that Miss Vernon behaved anything but correctly," Julien went on, "and indeed I was not, as your guest implied to me so mockingly, kissing her."

"Then perhaps you would care to explain what you were doing."

"I was saying 'goodbye'," Julien Wilsdon replied miserably. "My father has forced me, much against my wish, to join the Army. I am leaving today. And because I love Clarinda, I came to bid her 'farewell'."

Lord Melburne said nothing and after a moment Julien continued,

"It was unmanly of me, my Lord, but I was almost in tears. And when I put my cheek against Clarinda's, as a brother might do to his sister, she did not repulse me. That is all – I am telling you the truth because I would not have you think that she is anything but *perfect*.

He turned towards the door as he finished speaking and Lord Melburne had the idea that he was fighting to control himself.

"Thank you, Wilsdon, I am much obliged for your explanation," he said quietly.

Then realising how humiliating it must have been for the boy, for he was little more, to apologise, he added kindly,

"Good luck in the Army. You will enjoy it, even though you don't think so now. I swear to you the happiest days of my life were when I was with my Regiment."

"I do hope you are right, my Lord," Julien Wilsdon said despondently and went from the room, closing the door quietly behind him.

Lord Melburne waited just a few moments until he thought that Julien would have left the house before he went from the salon into the hall.

Bates was standing by the door.

"Lady Romayne Ramsey left you her compliments, my Lord, and asked me to tell your Lordship that she would wait for you at Melburne."

"Then I will follow her Ladyship right away. Will you give Sir Roderick my respects and say an unexpected guest precludes my being able to visit him at the time I intended. But I will return later this evening at about an hour before dinner."

"Very good, my Lord."

Lord Melburne hesitated a moment and then he added,

"And tell Miss Vernon I would be deeply obliged if I might dine with her this evening. It will be too late after I have finished with Sir Roderick for me to return home for dinner."

"I will tell Miss Clarinda, my Lord," the butler said. "I hope we shall be able to offer your Lordship a meal to your satisfaction."

Lord Melburne went towards his phaeton with a twinkle in his eyes. He was certain it would infuriate Clarinda to be forced to entertain him.

But he knew that the fact he was dining out would provide him with a plausible excuse to send Lady Romayne back to London.

Also he could not deny it that he wanted to see Clarinda again.

CHAPTER FOUR

Clarinda reached the sanctuary of her bedroom and slammed the door behind her.

She stood for a moment with her hands to her flushed face, conscious that her heart was beating violently in her breast and she was angry with a fury that she had never experienced before.

"How dare he! *How dare he!*" she cried aloud and, stamping her foot as she had stamped it at Lord Melburne, she ran across the room to fling herself down onto her bed and bury her face in the pillow.

She had known, she now told herself, when Sir Roderick had first made her write and ask Lord Melburne to come to The Priory, that this was bound to happen.

It was exactly how she had anticipated that he would behave and yet the realisation was so different from her imaginings.

She had no idea that a man's lips could be so hard and fierce as Lord Melburne's had been when he had first kissed her and she had never dreamt that the same lips could become persuasive yet gentle and possessive yet tender.

So that was being kissed!

His Lordship behaved in the same licentious manner that she had expected and she had been ready for him. Ready with the speech that she had rehearsed to herself a hundred times because there was every chance that with such a near neighbour she would meet him sooner or later.

"He is despicable," she shouted out aloud. "I hate him! *I hate him*!"

As she spoke, she knew that the hatred that she had felt for him for the last four years was now far more violent and real because he had the power to disturb her personally.

It was not only what he said, it was those strange grey eyes of his which seemed to look deep into her heart and which made her feel small and unsure of herself.

She felt, when he came into a room being so incredibly handsome, so immaculate and fashionably dressed, that she paled into insignificance in her shabby gowns and with her hair arranged untidily and her total ignorance, of which she was very conscious, of the fashionable world.

Why should he perturb her so greatly?

She hoped that Sir Roderick would not live long and then Lord Melburne would depart back to London and she need never see him again.

"I hate him! *I hate him*!" she flashed again, thinking of his mouth on hers.

She rubbed her lips, but she knew that she could never entirely rub away the memory of her first kiss, a kiss that had ended almost sweetly.

It had given her the strangest feeling that, if she now surrendered herself to what Lord Melburne was asking of her with his lips, she would have lost her very identity.

She did not know quite what she meant, she had felt imprisoned by the strength of his arms and so small and so weak that it was almost impossible to fight him.

There was something he was demanding of her, something he was attempting to make her give him and something that he must take and hold captive!

She had the uneasy feeling that it was her heart.

'He had no right to touch me,' she told herself fiercely and yet she knew in all fairness that she had provoked him into excusable anger.

It must have been galling for him, she admitted, to find her with Julien and he was not to know that she was merely comforting a miserable young man who was near to tears because he must say 'goodbye'.

It was provoking enough for his Lordship to see them, but Clarinda did realise that the presence of a friend with him made it positively humiliating. She had heard a woman's voice and heard her laugh, an affected Society laugh, she thought scornfully and then she recalled the quick glimpse of a peaked bonnet, of floating plumes and a pelisse of vivid scarlet silk before she had turned and run for the shelter of the shrubbery.

Her face burnt at the thought. How could she have been so foolish?

She could have retained her composure and walked forward to greet the new guest to The Priory and explained that Julien was an old friend saying 'goodbye' before he joined the Army.

'Why,' she asked miserably, 'could I not have behaved like a lady instead of a child?'

She buried her face again in the pillow, ashamed at the mistake she had made. She told herself she could forgive Lord Melburne his anger, but he had kissed her and that she could never forgive.

'He is entirely unscrupulous where women are concerned,' she told herself harshly.

She remembered Jessica's soft voice telling her how she had fought against him until physically she was too exhausted to withstand his supreme strength. Later she had fought against her heart until it betrayed her into loving him.

Clarinda could recall all too clearly the horror that she had felt as Jessica Tansfield had unfolded her tale. Clarinda had been fifteen at the time, full of admiration of her grown-up friend, who past seventeen, was a *debutante* and had been presented to Their Majesties.

Jessica was pretty with her dark hair, her winged eyebrows and her slanting dark eyes. But, as she was bored in the country, she had made a confidante of little Clarinda, boasting of her many conquests, keeping her wide-eyed with stories of the fashionable world, of the routs and masques, the assemblies and balls, a world where apparently gentlemen stalked a pretty woman as if she was a wild animal they must capture and tame.

Then Jessica related how she had met Lord Melburne and he had ravished her against her will.

"Afterwards I loved him," she said with tears in her eyes. "I could not help it! I flung myself down at his feet and begged him to marry me, but he only laughed. Yes, he laughed, Clarinda, and I could only lie there, broken and desolate, my long hair then hanging over my shoulders to hide my nakedness."

Clarinda had felt even in that poignant moment of confession that Jessica was taking poetical licence for her hair had never grown longer than shoulder length.

But the story of Lord Melburne's brutality had made Clarinda swear undying enmity towards the man who had treated a young and innocent girl so callously.

"I gave him my body, my heart and my soul," Jessica sobbed brokenly. "I could not help it."

"Has anyone ever resisted him?" she asked Jessica.

"No one," Jessica replied, "because he is irresistible. That is what he is called in London and it is exactly what he is, Clarinda, irresistible. Poor weak women cannot escape from his magnetism and the power he exerts over every female he encounters."

Jessica had left The Priory to partake of the further gaiety and amusements of London, but Clarinda had stayed in the country and planned how she would behave if ever she might be unfortunate enough to meet Lord Melburne.

She would be completely unresponsive towards him, she told herself. It would be hard for a man to kiss a woman who was as cold as an iceberg in his arms.

The speech she had prepared would show him her utter contempt and she had rehearsed it over and over until she was word perfect.

She told herself now that she had recited it to perfection, except at the end when she had lost her temper and raged at him. This was perhaps because the tenderness of his kisses had been such a surprise.

In her anticipation of what would occur she had not expected him to be angry. He had held her close in his arms, but he had not made love to her as Jessica had described. Jessica had fought against his passionate desire and not his anger.

Clarinda recalled how roughly he had shaken her and she was certain that tomorrow she would have bruises on her shoulder.

Now she wondered who Lord Melburne's guest had been and what she and Julien might have said to each other when they were alone.

Clarinda felt herself blush again. How could she have been so gauche as to run away? She wondered what explanation Lord Melburne could have given the lady and whether they were still downstairs or if they had left The Priory.

Even as she wondered what had happened, there came a knock on her bedroom door. She sat up on the bed, tense and apprehensive. Then she realised that Lord Melburne would not knock so subserviently if he wished to enter her room.

"Come in," Clarinda called out.

Bates opened the door.

"His Lordship's compliments, Miss Clarinda," he announced, "and he has returned to Melburne. His Lordship asked me to tell you that he will visit Sir Roderick this evening and would be obliged if you would entertain him to dinner. It will be too late for him to return for dinner at Melburne after he has left Sir Roderick."

For a moment Clarinda could only stare at Bates.

How dare Lord Melburne invite himself to The Priory after the way he had behaved! But with a little lift of her chin she told herself that she was not afraid of him.

"Very well, Bates, tell cook to prepare a proper dinner for his Lordship's delectation."

"Very good, Miss Clarinda," Bates answered.

Then hesitatingly he said,

"I think I ought to tell you, miss, that the coachman to Lady Romayne Ramsey told me that the reason her Ladyship posted to Melburne is that Mr. Nicholas has heard about your betrothal to his Lordship. Mad as fire he is, according to her Ladyship's maid."

Clarinda gave a little cry.

"Oh, Bates, I hope Mr. Nicholas does not come here to upset Sir Roderick."

"I hope not indeed, miss," Bates replied before he closed the door.

When he had gone, Clarinda thought of Nicholas and her eyes were frightened. Nicholas at this very moment was as mad as fire as well because he knew he had been disinherited and that she, Clarinda, was to be the heir to the Priory Estates!

As she thought of him, Clarinda became aware that she was trembling. She felt hatred towards Lord Melburne, but her feelings about Nicholas were very different. Distrust of him had overshadowed her life ever since she had first seen him.

It had started when she first came to The Priory after her father and mother's death in a carriage accident. The curricle that Lawrence Vernon was driving collided with a mail coach and the lighter vehicle rolled down a steep incline and into a rocky stream. When the rescuers found them, both Lawrence Vernon and his wife were dead.

Sir Roderick Vernon had come to their home to take Clarinda away so that she could live at The Priory with him. He was a kind man and she soon developed a deep affection for him.

But she could see Nicholas, who had been abroad, striding into the salon unexpectedly and, although at first she was pleased to welcome a grown-up and elegant young man as a companion, she soon felt embarrassed by the expression in his eyes when he looked at her and by the way his hands sought excuses to touch her immature body.

She then found herself shrinking from his very proximity. She had tried to avoid him and made excuses not to be alone with him.

One night after she had gone to bed, she had heard someone open the door and thought it was the housekeeper or one of the housemaids. Then by the light of the candle burning by her bed she had seen Nicholas come creeping into the room, had observed the expression on his face and, innocent though she was, she knew that she was in deadly danger.

He had come nearer and nearer to her bed with a look in his eyes that made her scream in a terror that was based on instinct, an instinct that told her he was evil.

Her screams had brought Sir Roderick into the room. She had jumped from her bed into his arms sobbing bitterly and Nicholas's blustering lies had made no impression on his father.

Sir Roderick had heard far too many stories of his son's behaviour with young women. There was the tale of a farmer's daughter who was with child and innumerable other scandals that had reached Sir Roderick's ears from time to time.

But finding him in Clarinda's room had made him angry as Nicholas had never seen him angry before.

When Nicholas next returned after a six months' absence to The Priory, he paid little attention to Clarinda except to sneer at her and tell her sarcastically that she was 'the cuckoo in his nest'. But she was careful where possible to keep out of his sight and never to be alone with him.

Then three months ago he had come home after his father had been taken ill.

"I need money," he pronounced roughly to Clarinda. "How much have you got hidden away?"

"I have no money," Clarinda replied.

"I don't want your ribbon-pennies," Nicholas answered rudely, "you have the key to the rents and other income sales from the estate."

"But you cannot take those!" Clarinda almost screamed at him.

He wrenched the key from her when she tried to hide it from him, emptied the strongbox and laughed when she tried to dissuade him.

"Why not run tale-telling to my father?" he jeered, knowing that she would not upset Sir Roderick when he was so ill.

The next morning, when to Clarinda's relief Nicholas had announced he was returning to London, she found him in the library with a picture in his hand. It was a Van Dyck, which Sir Roderick had told her was very valuable and a family heirloom.

"What are you doing?" she asked before she could prevent the question.

"Helping myself to what is already mine or will be in a very short time," he answered.

"But you cannot take it while your father is still alive," she protested.

He looked at her with hard eyes, but his lips smiled.

"You cannot stop me!"

"No indeed, I have no right to do so," she replied, "but you must see what you are doing is wrong, even though it will be yours one day."

"What a little prude you are!" he exclaimed.

He put down the picture and stood looking at her.

"I think perhaps I would be wise to marry you," he said slowly. "You can spend your time here looking after the estate, which I understand you are most competent to do and I can amuse myself in London. I am sure you would be a most conformable wife."

"I have no desire to marry you," Clarinda answered quickly, "that is, if you are serious in what you suggest, which I doubt."

"I am serious," he replied. "Yes, it is a good idea. You have been growing very attractive these last few years, Clarinda. That untouched look has a charm of its own."

Then as he spoke his eyes narrowed and Clarinda felt a sudden awareness of evil.

She would have turned away and left the library, but he caught hold of her arm.

"A virgin," she heard him saying almost beneath his breath as if he had just thought of it.

"Let me go," she cried in a sudden panic.

"Afraid of me," he asked. "Well, why not? Fear can often be a very effective stimulus to desire."

"I don't know what you are talking about," Clarinda said. "Let me go, I think your father has need of me."

"And so have I!" Nicholas muttered, "so have I."

He released her and she then ran from the room, but, as she went, she knew that she was more afraid of him then than she had ever been of anyone in her whole life.

Very shortly after that she became aware of rumours and scandal about Nicholas. At first she had no idea what they sprang from, but from remarks made by the servants and the fact that Sir Roderick was unusually kind to her, she knew that Nicholas had committed some crime or sin that was unforgivable.

It did not surprise her, she had always known that he was wicked and she remembered again her terror when he had come to her room and when in the library he had talked about marriage.

Perhaps all men were wicked, she thought, perhaps all men were despicable, ruthless and brutal. She hated Nicholas and she hated Lord Melburne. Were they typical of their sex, so that a woman with any decency must stay away from all men?

Even though Clarinda might reiterate it again and again that she hated Lord Melburne, nevertheless, being a woman she could not resist attempting to look her best for him as she changed for dinner.

Her choice of gowns was not that large. She had three evening dresses, but they had now been in her wardrobe for years and were those which Sir Roderick had bought her only when the gowns she had brought with her from her home were too tight to be decent.

Sir Roderick hated spending money on anything but his beloved estate, so while Clarinda longed for new clothes, she was too fond of him to plague him to spend his money when she knew that he grudged her every penny of it.

She wished now, however, that she had one really smart and fashionable gown to dazzle Lord Melburne with for she knew how elegant he would be. It was amazing that he could dress so fashionably and yet not in any way appear to be a dandy.

She had thought that Julien looked very smart, but that was before she had seen Lord Melburne. Never had she imagined a man could have coats that fitted him without a wrinkle, or cravats so meticulously tied that they seemed to adorn him by nature and not artifice.

She looked with dissatisfied eyes at the three plain gowns that she must make her choice from. Finally she chose one of pale green, which she knew would make her skin seem white and bring out the red of her hair. It was a plain little dress made by the village seamstress, but Clarinda had added some satin ribbons to it.

When she was ready, she looked at her reflection in the mirror. Picking two white roses from the vase on her dressing table, she pinned them onto her dress and thought that, as she had no jewellery, they would relieve the plainness of her gown.

She had dressed more quickly than she anticipated and realised that it would be an hour before Lord Melburne would arrive to see Sir Roderick. Although she felt shy, she also felt a strange excitement at the thought of seeing him again.

He was her adversary, but there was something stimulating in pitting her wits against his.

He might even kiss her against her will, but he could not force her to tell him why she had such a dislike of him.

She knew it irritated and puzzled him not to know what she held against him and that her silence in keeping him guessing was a subtle revenge in itself.

At least life is different, not dull and uneventful, she thought as she ran down the stairs.

She decided that she would tidy the salon, as the housemaids often omitted to do, and see if Bates had thought to put out a bottle of Sir Roderick's best brandy.

She opened the door of the salon and stood frozen by fear into stillness.

Standing on the hearthrug with another man beside him was Nicholas.

"Good evening, Clarinda," Nicholas began.

She felt herself shrink inside at the sound of his voice and the look in his eyes, but she held her head proudly.

"Why are you here?" she managed to demand after a moment.

"I called to see you," Nicholas replied. "Bates told me you were changing for dinner so I told him not to disturb you. You have come downstairs quicker than I anticipated."

"We were not expecting you," Clarinda said, feeling that to speak more openly would be disloyal in front of a stranger.

Nicholas saw her glance at the man beside him and next he said,

"Gerald, allow me to present you to my father's niece. Sir Gerald Kegan – Miss Clarinda Vernon. Clarinda is to be my wife."

For a moment Clarinda was speechless and then she stated, stammering a little,

"It is not t-true! Why do you say s-such – things?"

"Because it just happens to be the truth," Nicholas answered. "I have come to fetch you, Clarinda. We are to be married later this evening."

"You must be crazed," Clarinda retorted. "You know full well I would never marry you."

Nicholas looked at her.

"I always felt you were dangerous, Clarinda, but your scheming is of little consequence because, when you are my wife, the estate will be mine and so will you."

Clarinda took a deep breath.

"Listen, Nicholas, I know that your father has disinherited you, leaving The Priory and the estate – to me, but I assure you I don't intend to keep it. It is yours by right and I intend to give you the greater part of what Uncle Roderick leaves me. There are certain cottages for old age pensioners and retired estate workers and a small house known as 'Four Gables' that I would like to keep. The rest is yours."

Nicholas twisted his lips.

"You are very accommodating when you are cornered, Clarinda, but I can assure you my way is the best. There will be no arguments then about who gives the orders."

"Do you really think I will agree to marry you?" Clarinda asked and now the loathing she had for him was evident in her voice.

"I think later you will be grateful to me," Nicholas said and there was something sinister in the way he spoke. "What do you think, Gerald?"

Clarinda looked quickly at the man beside him as if she could expect some help from that quarter.

Sir Gerald Kegan was a man of about forty and she thought that she had never seen a more debauched face. There were lines under his eyes and a look that told her, inexperienced and innocent though she was, that here was a man steeped in vice and degradation.

She would have no help from him, she was sure of it.

"Miss Vernon will make a very lovely – wife," Sir Gerald said in answer to Nicholas's question. He paused before uttering the word *wife* as if he was thinking of something else.

"Fetch your cloak, Clarinda," Nicholas ordered, "my carriage is waiting outside."

"I am not coming with you," she said, making a movement as if she would retreat, but Nicholas took hold of her arm.

"Now listen, Clarinda, you are coming with me to the caves. I expect you have heard about them."

He felt her stiffen and saw the sudden horror in her eyes.

"When our meeting there this evening is finished, I intend to make you my wife," he continued. "Most young women who are initiated into the mysteries of our Society are not so fortunate as to receive an offer of marriage. But you are an exception because, of course, you are my father's heiress."

"What are you saying to me?" Clarinda asked him in a low frightened voice. "Let me go, Nicholas, you cannot mean this!"

"But I *do* mean it," he answered. "No one is going to take my birthright from me. No, Clarinda, I am not such a fool as you and my father apparently imagine. Now come quietly, or if you prefer it I will drug you. I think you would find it impossible to struggle when I have poured this down your white throat."

He pointed to a small bottle that Sir Gerald Kegan had just drawn from his pocket. It was a black bottle such as chemists frequently used for poison.

Clarinda gave a little cry of horror.

"Yours is the choice," he sneered.

Clarinda then felt a sense of utter helplessness. This could not be true! It could not be happening to her.

Who would help her?

She remembered that Lord Melburne was coming to dinner, but she would have been taken away by Nicholas before he arrived.

"Choose," Nicholas said sharply as she did not answer. "Will you come willingly or do I render you insensible?"

"I will – not be – drugged," Clarinda faltered, "I will come – with – you."

"I thought you would," he said with an unpleasant smile of triumph on his face.

He took his hand from her arm and Clarinda looked round wildly for a means of escape.

Nicholas's lips jeered as he said,

"I was once a good runner, even though I am out of practice. And if you scream for help, who will come to your aid but old Bates, whom I could overcome with no effort or perhaps a giggling housemaid whom I omitted to seduce on my last visit here?"

Clarinda felt like screaming, but some inner pride would not allow her to give Nicholas the satisfaction of seeing her lose control of herself.

"I have told you – I will come with – you," she said, "I will not attempt to – run away."

"Come then," Nicholas ordered her.

With a mocking gesture he then offered her his arm. She took it feeling like the French aristocrats must have felt when they went to the guillotine.

As they reached the door of the salon, Nicholas suggested,

"You can send for your cape. I cannot allow you to go and get it yourself in case you have any foolish ideas of escape."

They went into the hall. Bates was standing by the front door and Clarinda saw the worry and anxiety in his old face. She was about to speak to him, when she saw Betty, her maid, who had come with her to The Priory, hovering at the top of the stairs.

Clarinda raised her voice.

"Betty," she said, "please bring me my cape from my bedroom, you know, the one with the hood."

"Very good, Miss Clarinda," Betty answered.

There was a tremor in her voice and Clarinda realised that, because Nicholas had been forbidden to come to The Priory, they knew that his presence was an outrage against their Master's wishes.

Betty came hurrying back with the cloak to where Clarinda was waiting with Nicholas and Sir Gerald, who were standing on either side of her. She turned her back on Betty, who placed the cloak over her shoulders and then quickly she turned round to say,

"My roses have come undone, fasten them securely for me."

Just for a moment she had her back to Nicholas and in a whisper, so that only Betty could hear her, she said,

"Tell his Lordship, the caves."

Then she turned, pulling her cloak around her and holding her head high she walked over the hall and out to the coach that was waiting outside. She felt numb, everything was unreal as in a distorted dream.

It was a large and luxurious carriage, she noticed with some detached part of her brain. The back seat was wide and the two men sat on either side of her, Nicholas on her right and Sir Gerald on her left.

She felt that she was a prisoner and they were her warders. She knew too that Sir Gerald deliberately sat as close as possible, his knee against hers. She felt revolted by him and again was conscious of a terrifying evil emanating from both men.

"I must congratulate you," Nicholas said as the horses started up, "on an admirable show of self-control, my dear Clarinda. I am surprised at your restraint."

"So am I," Sir Gerald agreed.

He put out his hand as he spoke and, taking Clarinda by the chin, turned her face round to his.

"She is lovely, very lovely," he said. "It's a pity, Nicholas, that I cannot be the first. You would not like, I suppose, to relinquish your authority as Master and give me the privilege of initiating this attractive creature into the delights of love."

Clarinda tried to twist her chin away from him, but he was too strong for her.

"Clarinda is to become my wife," Nicholas replied.

Sir Gerald glanced towards him.

"You might well change your tune by the time the night is over," he said. "Remember what happened to the last one when the others had finished with her."

"Clarinda will be my wife," Nicholas repeated.

"But at the moment she is unspoiled, entrancing and desirable," Sir Gerald murmured.

He bent his head towards Clarinda, his fingers still holding her captive. She realised that he was about to kiss her and with a quick movement of her body shrank away in terror from his thick lips, his coarse face and the glitter of lust in his eyes.

"Leave her alone!" Nicholas said sharply. "She is dedicated. She is the first one who we can be sure is pure and untouched. Tonight, He will come to us, I am convinced of it."

Reluctantly Sir Gerald set Clarinda free. She did not understand what they were saying and yet she knew that every word was impregnated with evil.

She wanted to scream out and scream again.

The numbness that seemed to have fallen on her like a cloud as she entered the coach was giving way to a horror that was terrifying her to the point when she knew her self-control might snap at any moment.

Only the knowledge that Nicholas would not hesitate to pour the obnoxious liquid down her throat made her keep still and silent.

The only hope of escape, she told herself desperately, was for her to keep her senses. There was just a chance that Lord Melburne might save her. How he would do it she did not know, but she found a strange comfort in thinking of his strength, of that firm squareness of his chin and the determination of his mouth.

She had seen him deal effectively with the bullying tenant who Nicholas had sent to The Priory and she felt that he would also be able to deal with Nicholas. Besides she had always been told it was impossible for anyone to better Lord Melburne in any activity. Had not his prowess at shooting, boxing and riding been a continual spur to her hatred of him because he was invariably so successful?

They drove relentlessly along the highway and she tried to remember all she had heard of the Hell Fire Clubs, but for the moment her memory seemed blank.

Then she realised that to enter a Club one must be a member. So just how would it be possible for Lord Melburne to rescue her if he could not effect an entrance?

With a sinking of her heart she felt that even if he had the support of the local people, it would be too late as far as she was concerned. She was both innocent and ignorant, but she had a vague idea why people spoke with bated breath about the orgies that took place in such Clubs.

Betty had told her that Simple Sarah had a child which had been fathered by Nicholas, a child that later had been stolen and, it was believed, had died in the caves. Clarinda had been shocked and she had not wanted to hear anymore.

But now she wished she had listened. Perhaps it would be better to be prepared for what lay ahead than just to trying to guess what horrors were waiting for her in the dark place.

They turned off the main highway and proceeded along the chalk road that led towards the caves. Clarinda had ridden that way in the past. Through the window she had a sudden glimpse of Dene's Farm and she knew as she saw it why Nicholas had wanted the new tenant to have it.

The man was a Priest, Clarinda was sure that she had been right in her supposition. It was he who would marry them, if indeed she was, as Nicholas had threatened, to become his wife when the ceremonies were over.

Why, why if she was to bear his name did he threaten to subject her to what she guessed would be a degradation and an outrage beyond words? Then she realised that Nicholas would never forgive her for stealing, as he thought, his inheritance from him.

He did not care for his home, he had never shown the least interest in the estate.

But it meant money, money for his depravity in London, money he would spend on his vices and gambling, money of which he never had enough, to be thrown away in a spendthrift fashion.

Impulsively Clarinda turned towards him.

"Nicholas," she said, "believe me, everything that your father has willed to me – will be yours. I give you my word, I will sign any papers you like. I will not take one penny of your money. Please don't do this to me. Let me free – I beg of you."

"Why should I?" Nicholas retorted. "Besides, even if I listened to your pleadings, which I have no intention of doing, I would not wish to disappoint my friends. How upsetting for everyone concerned for you not to play your part in the mysteries and not to participate in the ecstasy that Satan gives to all those who worship Him."

Could he really believe such nonsense? Clarinda wondered and then she remembered that she had once been told that Satanists were as fervent as Puritans.

The horses were slowing down as they approached the entrance to the caves.

"Do you really – credit," she whispered, "that you can evoke – the Devil Himself?"

"He will come to us tonight, I am sure of it," Nicholas replied and there was a note of madness in his voice that she had never heard before.

CHAPTER FIVE

Lord Melburne made no attempt to push his horses on the drive to his home. He wanted time to think and to be ready with an answer to the question that Lady Romayne was bound to ask him.

He felt a sudden surge of irritation to find himself in the position of having to give an explanation of what he believed until now was entirely his own business. At the same time he had to admit that, while it was interfering of Romayne to come posting down from London, she did have a certain amount of justification.

After all, whether he liked it or not, their names had been linked together and he knew the betting in St. James's was that Romayne would propel him up the aisle before the end of the year.

'*Blast it*, I want to remain a bachelor,' he told himself and then he found himself thinking of Clarinda and how soft her lips had been beneath his.

He was almost prepared to bet that it was the first time she had been kissed. There was an inexperience about her that was unmistakable. It was the first time, he thought, he had ever kissed anyone so young and so unsophisticated.

His love affairs had nearly always been with married women, mostly because they made it easy for him to accept their favours and also because, like many of his contemporaries, he found that women who were 'up to snuff' were far less dangerous than those who expected a Wedding ring in compensation for the surrender of their virtue.

Few married women in Society would dare risk the ostracism which must arise from being involved in a scandal. Few of them wished to incur their husband's wrath, which might even result in a duel, by being indiscreet where a lover was concerned.

But Romayne was different. Lord Melburne remembered uncomfortably that she was a widow. And although she undoubtedly came into the class of sophisticated females, there was no doubt at all that she would welcome another husband. And himself in particular.

How soft, how incredibly soft Clarinda's lips had been and yet she had not responded to his kisses, although he had tried most persuasively to make her yield.

He recognised how quickly most women would kiss him back with a wild abandon even before he himself was aroused, but the anger in Clarinda's eyes and the fury in her voice had told him all too clearly what emotion he had incited in her.

'I must be getting old,' he said to himself with a twist of his lips or was it that Clarinda was the type of female he had never met before, a cold and frigid woman?

That he could not believe, not with the colour of her hair.

He recalled the changing expressions on her face and the emotions that were so clearly expressed in her large eyes and the way her voice would sound quite passionate when she felt deeply about something. No, Clarinda was not cold. Except where he was concerned!

As he turned his horses into the great gates of Melburne with their heraldic stone lions standing Guardian on either side, he had the sobering thought that she had broken the legend of his irresistibility, which he had almost begun to believe in himself.

He had for the very first time in his life met a woman who did not find him irresistible, a woman who could keep a rigid control over herself that she had remained stiff and unyielding in his arms while her lips refused the invitation of his.

Anyway, why worry about her? As soon as Sir Roderick died, his involvement would end automatically, she would be rid of him and he of her. He had no wish, he told himself, to interfere where he was not wanted.

No, he would go back to London, amuse himself as he had always done and forget this tiresome country girl with her absurd dislike of him, which she would not substantiate.

Yet it was infuriating that his curiosity in the matter would remain unassuaged. He knew that this would be a constant irritation for him however much he tried to forget Clarinda.

Melburne looked very lovely in the late afternoon sunshine. The shadows were growing longer and clouds were drifting over the blue of the sky. The lake was molten silver, the wind was blowing among the purple and white lilac bushes and scattering the pink blossom from the almond trees.

It was breathtakingly beautiful, but for once Lord Melburne hardly noticed his home as he drove towards it for his thoughts were occupied elsewhere.

"Lady Romayne is in the Blue Salon, my Lord," the Major Domo told him as he entered the hall.

"I am dining out," Lord Melburne said, "and I wish to leave here in about an hour and a half. Order my closed carriage and two horses."

"Very good, my Lord."

Lord Melburne crossed the hall and entered the Blue Salon. Romayne was lying on the sofa with her head resting against a soft satin cushion as if she was tired. She had taken off her bonnet and her pelisse and she looked very beautiful with the transparency of her gauze dress revealing her sinuous figure, her red lips pouting a little, and her eyes hinting at unshed tears.

One white hand fluttered out towards him.

"Buck, my dear, how sweet of you to return so swiftly."

He bowed over her hand, but did not touch it with his lips. Then he stood, his arm on the mantelpiece, looking down at her.

"I know what you are going to ask me," he began, "and quite frankly, Romayne, I have no explanation to give you at the moment. In a day or two perhaps, but now I have nothing to say."

She clasped her hands together.

"You are being cruel to me," she complained. "You are telling me that I should not have come to see you, that I should have stayed in London beset by anxiety, worried and distressed because you had not confided in me. Oh, my dear cousin, why do you not trust me?"

"It is not a question of trust," Lord Melburne replied.

"You are prevaricating," Lady Romayne said accusingly. "You know as well as I do that something untoward has occurred. But I will not badger you, I am far too sensible for that. All I want to know, and please be truthful, is everything – finished between – us?"

There was a little sob in her voice.

She turned her head aside as though she must hide her tears from him.

"Surely that is presuming many things that I am not prepared to admit," Lord Melburne said. "There has never been anything between us, Romayne, except what I believe to be a warm friendship."

"It may have been only friendship on your part, Buck," she replied, "but on mine it was very – different."

"If that is true," he said, "this is not the time or the place, Romayne, to discuss it. Please do as I ask of you. Don't try to force me into giving you an explanation that I cannot proffer at this particular moment, but which will quite easily be yours within a week."

"Why, why are you entangled?" Romayne asked, her voice rising. "Who is this country wench, this badly dressed and badly-behaved young woman who, if she has not captured your fancy, has at least involved you in a situation that must puzzle, if not perturb, your friends like myself?"

"My friends like yourself were not supposed to hear about it," Lord Melburne said. "This is entirely a local problem, Romayne, which should not have gone beyond the gates of The Priory and the gates of Melburne. It is something that involves the wishes of a dying man and that is all I can tell you at the moment."

"If you had told me that personally in private," Lady Romayne answered, "I would, of course, have accepted your confidence gladly and helped you if you needed my help. But for Mr. Nicholas Vernon, whom I hardly know, to announce your betrothal in my own drawing room when I was entertaining friends is hardly something that you would expect me to accept calmly and without question."

"You could have questioned me when I return to London," Lord Melburne said a little coldly.

"And when is that likely to be?" Lady Romayne asked. "I called at Melburne House and they told me they expected you yesterday. When I sent round again this morning and found you had not returned, I felt the only thing was to come to Melburne and find out for myself what was so momentous as to keep you in the country."

Lord Melburne said nothing and after a moment Lady Romayne continued softly,

"To set my mind at rest, Buck, tell me something that will make me happy. Tell me our relationship is the same as it has ever been and that at least you care for me – a little."

"I don't know quite what you mean?" Lord Melburne replied evasively. "As I have already told you, our relationship, as far as I am concerned, is one of friendship. On many occasions we have enjoyed each other's company. I hope that will continue."

Lady Romayne rose from the sofa and moved towards him. When she reached his side she held out her hand.

"You know," she said softly, "that I want more than that."

He did not touch her, he only looked down at her dark beauty, her long lashes fluttering against her cheeks and her red lips raised invitingly towards his.

"I think, Romayne," he said quietly, "it is time for you to return to London. I am dining out and I have an appointment before dinner. There is not time to discuss anything now."

She moved a little nearer to him and put out one hand to touch him.

"And suppose," she said in a very soft voice, "I feel too exhausted to return to London tonight? Suppose I stay with you here at Melburne. Would that be very – compromising?"

His Lordship's eyes were hard and the lines round his mouth seemed more cynical than usual as he answered,

"Not in the least, my dear Romayne. If you want to stay here, it can be arranged. My Agent, Major Foster, who you may remember, has a charming wife who will, I am sure, act as your chaperone if I ask her to do so. The Fosters could entertain you at dinner and if, as I suspicion, I will not be too late, we might have a game of cards when I return."

Lady Romayne turned away from Lord Melburne with a decided flounce. And there was a petulant note in her voice as she responded,

"I would not put you to such inconvenience. I will return to London and I hope that this explanation you have promised me will not be too long in coming. But Heaven knows your friends who will have learnt of your betrothal will be filled with considerable curiosity as to the appearance and behaviour of the young woman who has captured the heart of the *Beau Ton's* most perennial bachelor."

"How many people has Nicholas Vernon told?" Lord Melburne asked in a sharp voice.

Lady Romayne shrugged her shoulders.

"I have not the slightest idea," she replied. "Why should I?"

"How did it happen that he told you?" Lord Melburne said. "I had no conception that you knew him."

Before Lady Romayne could answer, the door opened and the butler and two footmen appeared with a silver tray, tea and coffee, a number of cakes and sweetmeats, which they arranged on a table beside the sofa with dignity and what was to Lord Melburne an irritating slowness.

"I hope you don't mind. Buck, my having asked for some refreshment?" Lady Romayne smiled. "I left London after an early and light luncheon."

"My apologies that I had not thought of it myself," Lord Melburne replied.

The butler and footmen, having arranged everything with a pernickety precision, left the room and Lady Romayne opened the Queen Anne silver canister that contained tea.

"Can I offer you anything, Buck?" she asked him, conscious that she looked very lovely busying herself with what was essentially a feminine task.

"No thank you," Lord Melburne answered.

"You know, Buck, if I am frank with you," Lady Romayne said in her sweetest voice, "I have always thought that you need a chatelaine at Melburne. It is a very beautiful house, but it requires a woman's touch. What is more, when you do marry, if you are to have peace of mind, you will need as a wife someone who you are certain is marrying you for yourself and not for your money or your title."

"These things have crossed my mind," Lord Melburne replied.

Lady Romayne spooned the tea into the teapot and poured the boiling water into it from a silver water jug.

"I am really quite hungry," she said, reaching out her hand for a tiny sponge cake that looked so light that a puff of wind might have blown it away.

"Do you realise, Buck," she continued, "if you do not return tomorrow, you will miss Prinny's party at Carlton House and that will annoy him because he is exceeding fond of you, as you well know."

"Is he giving another of those overheated crushes?" Lord Melburne asked in his most uncompromising voice.

"Yes indeed. And he has some new pictures to show us. He will be most piqued if you are not there."

Lord Melburne walked to the window looking out towards the lake. The sun had gone in, clouds had overcast the sky and there was a sudden shower of rain beating down on the lawns and the lake.

The storm held a beauty all of its own and, as he watched it, he thought how infinitely he preferred to be at Melburne than to be fighting his way through the overcrowded throng that would fill Carlton House to stupefaction the following evening.

He could see the Prince of Wales's guests all too clearly, the over-jewelled women with their transparent gowns, the men cluttered with decorations, the chatter of high voices and the tinkle of laughter which was so often malicious and unkind.

He would know them all, each and every one of them, by name and yet were they really his friends? What did they really mean to him? He felt a sudden boredom creep over him, the boredom he had experienced so often and, as he was aware of it, he knew too that he was bored with Romayne.

Just for a very short period he had contemplated that he might marry her. It had been so obviously the right thing to do. He had even imagined the Prince of Wales at their Wedding, perhaps taking it upon himself with one of his gracious gestures to give away the bride.

It would have been a popular marriage, a marriage that everyone would approve of and now he knew it would never happen. Romayne bored him as so many other women had bored him in the past. She was beautiful, but he felt that there was nothing behind her beauty. Yet what did he expect from a woman?

What was he looking for?

Why was he continually disappointed?

He looked out on the rain, saw the wind blowing ripples across the lake and had a sudden desire to go out of doors to feel the roughness of the elements.

He wanted to get away from the softness of white hands and yielding bodies, away from voices that spoke to him caressingly and eyes that looked at him yearningly.

He wanted to battle against something, he wanted to meet some challenge that demanded his whole strength although how and why he did not know.

He was suddenly aware that Romayne had left the tea table and was standing beside him.

"We could be so very happy, Buck dear," she said almost beneath her breath. "If only you would stop being elusive and running away from the inevitable."

It was the last word that made Lord Melburne stiffen and say almost sharply,

"You have not yet answered my question, Romayne. How did you learn from Nicholas Vernon that I was betrothed to his father's niece?"

"He came to my house yesterday evening," she replied automatically, as if she realised that the moment for sentiment had passed and she could not force it upon Lord Melburne.

"I had no conception you knew him," Lord Melburne said again.

"Oh, I have met him on various occasions," Lady Romayne answered. "He was never a young man I had much partiality for, despite the fact that he is quite attractive in a dark and daredevil manner."

She glanced at Lord Melburne under her eyelashes as she spoke as if she hoped to make him jealous.

"Go on," Lord Melburne prompted.

"I was entertaining some friends," Lady Romayne said "There was Lady Snellsborough, Olivia Knightly, both friends of yours, and John Davies, Lord Down and Sir Gerald Kegan,"

"That outsider!" Lord Melburne expostulated. "Why did you invite him?"

"My dear Buck, he is very rich and gives the most amusing parties. I grant you he is not particularly prepossessing, in fact I always think that there is something sinister about him. Olivia thinks that he is the most depraved man she has met and she swears, although I don't believe she knows what she is talking about, that he is a Satanist,"

"Go on," Lord Melburne said sharply.

He was suddenly alert and his boredom had vanished. He was like a hunter who sees the tracks of his prey and knows that he must follow them.

"We were all talking," Lady Romayne continued, "when suddenly Nicholas Vernon was announced. I looked up in surprise, I really was astonished to see him. He had never called on me before."

"What did he say?" Lord Melburne enquired.

"He bowed over my hand, apologised for intruding and said he had long been meaning to pay his respects, but was not certain of my address. I had a suspicion, of course, that this was not true and he had another reason for coming, but all I could do was to smile and introduce him to my friends. Then I heard him saying in a low voice, which he did not think I could overhear, to Sir Gerald Kegan,

"'I was told I would find you here'."

"What else did he say?" Lord Melburne demanded.

"You know, Buck, I have very acute hearing," Lady Romayne said. "I had crossed the room to the bell-pull, which was quite near to them. I heard Nicholas Vernon continue, 'I am arranging a special meeting tomorrow night. Something has occurred that makes it imperative to hold one.' 'Tomorrow night?' Sir Gerald said in that unpleasant voice of his, which, I do not know why, always makes me shudder."

"What else did he say?" Lord Melburne asked impatiently.

"He added," Lady Romayne continued, 'I shall be there, Nicholas.' 'So I must tell the others,' Nicholas Vernon told him, 'and I do promise you, Gerald, it will be a very special meeting. Incidentally I shall need your help, so drive down with me.' 'And our Venus, is she lovely?' Sir Gerald then asked. 'You will find her exquisite and completely – untouched,' Nicholas replied."

Lord Melburne did not speak and Lady Romayne went on,

"Then they moved apart and Nicholas Vernon, lifting my hand to his lips, suddenly said in a loud voice,

"'I must now leave you, my Lady, but before I go I have some information that I feel will be of interest to you.'

"He looked at me with those dark eyes of his and I had the feeling he was deliberately being unpleasant, that he desired to hurt me and make me unhappy.

"'What is it?' I enquired'."

"'I have just learnt the news,' he replied, 'that your cousin is affianced to my father's niece – Clarinda Vernon.'

"'My cousin?' I asked and as I spoke I knew what the answer would be.

"'Yes, your cousin – Lord Melburne,' he said. 'His estates march with mine. I shall be seeing him tomorrow, shall I offer him your congratulations?'"

Lady Romayne's expression darkened.

"He was being deliberately cruel, Buck, I knew it. He was just trying to make me look foolish in front of my friends, He knew we had been talked about, you and I, and he wished to humiliate me."

"What did you say?" Lord Melburne asked.

"For a moment I was speechless," Lady Romayne answered, "and then, as he walked to the door, he looked back and laughed, an unpleasant laugh, a mocking one and a sound I can hardly describe.

~102~

"'Yes, they are affianced,' he said, 'but it will not be for long'."

"Are you sure that is exactly what he said?" Lord Melburne said and his tone was harsh and insistent.

"Yes, I am quite sure," Lady Romayne said. "I have told you exactly what happened."

"Then listen," Lord Melburne said and he had a purposeful air about him. "I must leave at once. Go back to London, I cannot wait to see you off. I cannot explain, but I assure you it is of the utmost import."

"Why, Buck, why?" Lady Romayne enquired, her voice rising almost shrilly.

Then she realised that, without even waiting to answer her, Lord Melburne had left the room and she was now alone in the Blue Salon.

Lord Melburne hurried across the hall.

"My carriage," he demanded, "I need my carriage immediately."

"I ordered it for six o'clock, my Lord," the butler told him

"I must leave now," Lord Melburne said. "Send someone to fetch it."

The butler snapped his fingers and one of the footmen ran through the door and hurried off towards the stables.

"You will not be changing, my Lord?" the butler enquired.

"No," Lord Melburne answered, "there is no time."

He took his top hat, set it on his head and then stood tapping his foot impatiently until the closed carriage came hastily round from the stables.

He almost ran down the steps and reached the carriage door before the footman had time to open it.

"The Priory," he said sharply to the coachman, "and hurry!"

The horses were fresh and they took a comparatively short time to traverse the few miles that lay between the two houses. Lord Melburne was tense as he sat back against the soft-cushioned seat.

He wondered as they went whether he would be wise to get hold of Major Foster first. Then he realised with the instinct of a man who has been a soldier and planned his operations with an eye to detail that the first objective must be to make sure that Clarinda was still at The Priory.

It seemed absurd even to contemplate such an idea, but something had told him with a terrifying clarity that she was in appalling danger.

It was, of course, unthinkable that Nicholas, who after all had been born a gentleman, would involve Clarinda in the filth and degradation of his Hell Fire Club.

But he had said to Gerald Kegan, '*she is exquisite and untouched*'.

How many women did Nicholas know who came into that category?

Lord Melburne was aware that the woman who took part in the Ceremony of the Black Mass was referred to as 'The Venus'.

And she must by custom be pure and a virgin!

Lord Melburne thought of Sir Gerald Kegan and his fists clenched automatically. He was a lecher of the worst type, a man with such an unsavoury reputation that, unless he had been extremely wealthy, there would have been no lady's drawing room he could set foot in.

He remembered Sir Gerald had a reputation for liking very young girls. He had heard men laugh about him in the Club. He had heard him spoken about as being a frequenter of the bawdy houses that supplied their clients with maidens fresh from the country, often recruited by the despicable method of meeting stagecoaches at their London terminus.

An innocent young girl coming to London in search of employment would find herself bewildered and frightened by the noise and crowds. She was therefore only too glad to avail herself of the help proffered by some respectable-looking middle-aged woman who would whisk her away to a brothel before she had any idea of what was happening.

It was these notorious establishments that catered for the perverted tastes of gentlemen like Gerald Kegan and Nicholas Vernon. They were both, Lord Melburne thought, despicable characters, men without principle, without decency and without honour.

He clenched his hands until the knuckles showed white. He knew now only too well what Lady Romayne had described as an unpleasant look in Nicholas's eyes. And he was sure, as he had never been sure before, that the stories about the Hell Fire Caves were not exaggerated.

He had learnt now who paid for them. Kegan's wealth had been at Nicholas's disposal for the excavations, the furnishings and doubtless the food and wine that would be required in vast quantities for the type of companions who would wish to be members of such a Club.

It would have been Kegan's money that provided the wagonloads of women brought down London. Women who would do anything for gold and submit to whatever beastliness was required of them to satisfy gentlemen who could pay as well as Nicholas would be able to do with Kegan's backing.

'God, if only I had known of this before,' Lord Melburne exclaimed to himself.

Then he knew that, as he had said to Major Foster, he needed proof before he could act.

'But supposing,' some quiet voice within him asked, "supposing that the proof is to be Clarinda?"

'It is ridiculous, it is unthinkable,' his common sense replied and yet his instinct told him that Clarinda was in deadly danger.

She was innocent and exquisite and had undoubtedly incurred the enmity of Nicholas Vernon by becoming the heiress to the lands and fortune of which he had been disinherited.

'Why could I not have guessed something like this would happen?' Lord Melburne asked himself. 'I should have taken her away from The Priory, where there is only a dying man and a few old servants to protect her. I should have been on my guard as soon as I had learnt that a prying footman had carried a message to London.'

He had forgotten that he had told himself it was none of his business, forgotten that he did not wish to be involved and forgotten that only this morning he had decided that when Sir Roderick was dead his part would have been played and he would have no share or interest in Clarinda's future.

Now he knew that he must save her, save her from a peril so appalling that he could not even think of it clearly or put it into words.

The horses were moving at a quick pace, but he rapped on the glass window.

"Quicker," he demanded of the coachman, "go quicker."

They went down The Priory drive at a speed that made the lightly sprung coach rock as if it was on a rough sea. As they drew up at the entrance, Lord Melburne opened the carriage door and stepped out before the footman could get down from the box.

Bates was standing in the open doorway.

"Your Lordship, thank God you have come!"

"What has happened? Where is Miss Clarinda?" Lord Melburne demanded.

It was then Betty, who ran forward, tears running down her cheeks and her eyes red from crying.

"Oh, your Lordship, Mr. Nicholas has taken her away. She whispered to me as I put on her cloak, '*tell his Lordship, the caves*'."

"The caves," Lord Melburne repeated and knew it was what he had expected to hear. "How long since they left? Did Miss Clarinda go willingly?"

"I think she had no choice, my Lord," Betty said. "There was Mr. Nicholas and another gentleman, a middle-aged man who looked – if your Lordship will forgive me – a wicked person."

"I know who you mean," Lord Melburne nodded briefly.

"Miss Clarinda was very pale," Betty went on. "She held her head high, but I'm sure, my Lord, that she was frightened. She made an excuse that the roses on the front of her dress had come undone so that she could whisper to me, but her hands were tremblin' so that if they had been loose it would have been impossible for her to fasten them."

"How long since they left," Lord Melburne asked.

"About half an hour ago," Bates answered.

Lord Melburne, without a word, turned, ran down the steps and entered his coach.

"Where to, my Lord?" the footman enquired.

"Turn right when you leave the lodge gates," he said, "go down the road for about two miles and I will tell you when to turn off. And hurry!"

"Very good, my Lord."

The horses started off and Lord Melburne lay back in the coach. Those who had been with him in the War would have known by the set of his chin and the expression on his face that he was at his most formidable.

When the battle was at its fiercest and they were hard pressed, the men serving under him had always looked to Lord Melburne for a change of tactics, a different approach or a brilliant idea which would often turn defeat into a victory.

But Lord Melburne knew that this situation was something so difficult and unusual that for the moment it seemed to him that his brain was not working and he was stunned into a kind of vacancy that gave him no idea of what he must do or even an indication of the first steps he must take.

He was fully aware that Clubs such as Nicholas had in the chalk caves were not only conducted with utmost secrecy because their members were afraid of being exposed but were usually over-subscribed rather than in need of new associates. It would not be a question of bribing himself into the place nor of entering it by force.

He had seen the entrance when he visited it with Major Foster and he knew that one man with a pistol could keep a whole legion of intruders at bay without the slightest difficulty.

It would be no use blundering up to the place and demanding Clarinda. They could lock the gates and laugh at his endeavours to save her. And all the money in the world would not get him past the gatekeeper if the man was a loyal servant to Nicholas Vernon.

He thought of the brusqueness with which the Priest had refused to speak to him and he knew with a sudden despondency why a Priest was necessary and why Nicholas had insisted on his being given the tenancy of Dene's Farm. A discredited Priest who would perform the Black Mass and, if necessary, perform a marriage!

As for Clarinda, he hardly dared think of her and what she must be suffering. She was so young, so pitifully young and inexperienced.

She could never in her wildest dreams have possibly imagined the licentiousness of men dedicated to the worship of Satan, men in whom the last remnants of decency were dead, so that an innocent and untouched girl meant something very different to them from what she meant to other men.

'God save her,' Lord Melburne muttered beneath his breath and it was a prayer that came from the very depths of his heart.

CHAPTER SIX

As the carriage came to a stop, Nicholas and Sir Gerald Kegan drew black masks from their pockets and put them over their eyes.

It gave them a sinister appearance, which made Clarinda feel even more acutely than she had before that her self-control was on the verge of breaking and she would scream.

For one wild moment she thought, as she stepped from the coach, that she might run away.

But she knew that Nicholas had not boasted when he had said that he had been a good runner and the same pride that had come to her assistance at The Priory made her feel that she could not humiliate herself by trying to escape only to be recaptured in front of the servants.

"We are early," Sir Gerald Kegan remarked as they alighted.

Nicholas looked round to see only a very few carriages and a big covered wagon parked outside the caves.

"It will be extremely crowded later on," he replied. "Nearly everyone I have spoken to was determined to be present on this auspicious occasion."

He took Clarinda's arm and his eyes glittering through the mask made her feel that she was already in the presence of some devouring demon.

"The celebrated Wedding of the Master," he mocked, "Is something that every member wishes to celebrate."

She made no effort to reply to him. She felt as if her voice had died in her dry throat. A fear such as she had never before experienced was sweeping over her as

Nicholas led her through the great iron gateway behind which at a table sat a man in livery.

Clarinda had a glimpse of a pistol in his belt and she knew that it was to repel intruders. She felt despairingly that Lord Melburne would never get past him.

"Your badges, gentlemen?" the man in uniform asked and then added,

"I know you, Mr. Vernon."

But he put out his hand to Sir Gerald, who drew something from his waistcoat pocket, showed it and put it back again.

There were footmen in attendance as they went down the strange passageway which had been burrowed, as Clarinda recognised, out of the chalk rock.

Although it was hung with red velvet curtains and the floor was carpeted, the ceiling was left white and bare and occasionally on the red carpet beneath her feet Clarinda could see small pieces of chalk that had fallen down, as if to remind those who entered that they were going down deep into the bowels of the earth.

There were candles to light the way set in sconces, which were either fashioned in the grinning mask of some terrifying monster or so obscene in design that even if Clarinda had looked at them she would not have understood what they depicted.

The passageway descended sharply. Then there was the sound of voices and Nicholas led her through a doorway covered with a hanging curtain into what seemed a comparatively large room.

There was a woman standing in the centre of it and for a moment Clarinda had a gleam of hope as she realised that she was dressed as a nun. Then, as she heard

Nicholas address her familiarly, she realised that the face of the supposed nun was rouged and painted, her eyes mascaraed and her lips vermilion red.

"Good evening, Moll, my dear," Nicholas greeted her. "I was hoping you would be here in plenty of time. I have brought you the prettiest Venus you have ever seen."

He pulled Clarinda forward as he spoke and the woman's hard eyes flickered over her.

"Pretty enough!" she said in a common voice. "But they all starts like that."

"Prepare her now for the ceremony," Nicholas commanded. "Tell her what to expect and warn her to behave herself. If she is hysterical, drug her."

He turned as he spoke and looked back at Sir Gerald, who had followed them.

"You have the stuff, Gerald," he said, "give it to Moll."

"I thought Sir Gerald would be 'ere this evening," Moll said with an almost insolent note in her voice. "What part are you to play then in the evenin' activities, my fine gentleman, or needn't I ask the question?"

"Alas, mine is a merely subsidiary part," Sir Gerald replied. "The Master insists on his rights. But perhaps he will feel more generous-hearted before the evening is out."

"No," Nicholas said firmly, "I have told you why I intend to be the first. But I have no time to waste talking. Get on with your work, Moll. I have a deal to see to. Tonight is to be the most memorable night the Club has ever known, a night we shall all remember for the rest of our lives."

Again there was that note of mad elation in his voice as he turned and walked from the cave. Sir Gerald lingered a moment to press the black bottle containing the drug into Moll's hand.

Then he said in a low voice to her,

"Don't use this on the girl if you can help it. I may have need of it later."

There was a clink of coins and Clarinda saw him passing several sovereigns into Moll's eager hand at the same time as she took the bottle.

"Be a good girl," he said to Clarinda, "and do what our Abbess tells you. It will be a pity if she is obliged to render you insensible. You will find the ceremony, if nothing else, an enlightening experience."

His lips beneath the mask seemed to leer at Clarinda so that instinctively she shrank back from him and found herself touching the black habit which covered the Abbess.

When Sir Gerald disappeared, Clarinda said in a frightened whisper,

"Help me – *please help me* – if you have a shred of kindness anywhere in your heart, have – pity on me, for I have been brought here – against my will. If you will help me to escape, I can give you money – a lot of money. Five hundred pounds – a thousand, it does not signify. When my uncle dies – he is Mr. Vernon's father – I shall be very wealthy. I shall give you anything you ask if only you will – help me away from here."

Moll looked at her and Clarinda felt that there was some kindliness in her painted face. She was a middle-aged woman and the life she led had undoubtedly taken toll of her looks.

~113~

Once she must have been pretty. There was still a pale reflection of it in her appearance although it was almost obscured by her coarse blemished skin, the bags of fat under her eyes and the fallen contour of her chin.

"I know what you're feelin', child," she said. "I went through this many years ago when I were younger than you, not more than thirteen and pure and decent, although there'd been plenty after me. But they took me to the caves at West Wycombe. I remember goin' on my knees before Sir Francis Dashwood and pleadin' with 'im to spare me,"

"Then you understand," Clarinda said eagerly. "Please help me – *please*."

The woman called Moll shook her head.

"There's not an 'ope, dearie," she answered. "Even if you were to offer me one million golden guineas I couldn't get you away from 'ere. It isn't as though I wouldn't welcome the money, but no woman can leave the caves unless she be accompanied by a gentleman."

"Are you sure – quite sure?" Clarinda asked and her voice seemed choked in her throat.

"As sure as I be standin' 'ere," Moll answered her. "And the gentlemen who comes 'ere come for one thing only and you knows what that is."

"But I don't," Clarinda answered. "Mr. Vernon said that you were to tell me what – to expect. I would rather – know."

"It would be best if you didn't," Moll answered. "If you take my advice, you'll drink what's in this bottle, whatever that Sir Gerald says to the contrary. I can't stand that man, that be the truth for all that he's generous with 'is gold when it pleases him."

"I have no wish to be insensible," Clarinda protested.

"Then have a drink, dearie. Gin 'elps, I promise you. I'll get you a glass."

"No – *no*," Clarinda cried, "I want – nothing! Just tell me what I have to – do."

"'Tis the Black Mass, you've heard of it, I suppose?" Moll asked.

Clarinda knew then that at the back of her mind it was what she had always expected and what she had known must happen in the caves. She then remembered reading how Catherine Medici of France, wife of Henry II, had celebrated the Black Mass in her efforts to destroy her husband's affection for Diane Poitier.

She had read a description of what took place in French and she thought then that it was more descriptive, more frankly written than would have been allowed if the book had been printed in English.

"The Black Mass!"

She knew now without being told what part she was to play.

Venus was the naked woman who lay on the altar and over whom the Black Mass was blasphemously celebrated.

The knowledge came to her like a flash of lightning searing into her consciousness, making her feel sick and faint with the full implication of what it entailed. Trembling, she put her hands up to her face as if she would blot out the horror of what in her mind's eye she saw happening.

"You had best drink this, dearie," Moll said, holding out a glass half-full of neat gin as Clarinda stood there trembling. "They take you when the Service is finished, the Master first. But by that time they are drunk or drugged and you'll need somethin', you will really."

"What I shall need is not a drug," Clarinda replied in a slow voice.

She knew in that very moment that, if she was not rescued by the time the Service was finished, then there was only one thing she could do and that was to die.

There would be knives on the tables, she thought. Somehow she would seize one and kill herself before the final degradation could happen to her.

Quite clearly she could remember the place in which a knife's entry in the body could kill the victim almost immediately. She remembered her adopted father telling her about it when he was describing the way a gladiator who had been defeated was despatched by the victor when the Roman Emperor turned his thumb down.

It was the same place chosen by the Japanese when committing *hara-kiri* when they fell on their swords. Somehow she would get hold of a knife and somehow she would kill herself before Nicholas or any other man touched her.

It seemed to Clarinda, having made her decision, that she received a new strength. She took her hands from her face.

"Tell me," she said to Moll, "what happens – first?"

"You take off your clothes, dearie," Moll answered, "and I dress you in the white robe of Venus. While they dine you sit at the foot of the altar. No man touches you, you're dedicated to Satan 'imself."

Just for a moment Clarinda felt herself tremble.

"Do – do these ceremonies really evoke the – magic powers of the – underworld?" she asked.

Moll gave a laugh.

"If they do, I've seen no sight nor sign of 'em!" she replied. "But they that drinks a great deal or takes drugs swear they sees wondrous sights."

Clarinda gave a sigh of relief and then she knew that she had been wrong even to think that such a thing was possible. If she was to be saved, only one thing could save her – the power of good. God would not be mocked by perverts like Nicholas conjuring up devils for their own lustful self-satisfaction.

'I must pray,' she thought, 'pray as I have never prayed before that God in His mercy will send Lord Melburne to save me.'

How it was possible, having seen the entrance to the caves, how anyone could come to her rescue, she had no idea, but she only felt that while the terror within her was still there, she was not now on the verge of breaking down as she had been a little earlier.

Obediently, without protest, she went into the corner of the cave with Moll and started to take off her clothes. While she was doing it a number of other women arrived.

They wore flashy evening dresses, they were all smelling of cheap scent and chattering together in their coarse common voices. Most of them were young and attractive enough in a vulgar manner, but heavily painted, giggling and laughing at what lay ahead.

The majority of them donned nuns' robes and wore little, if anything underneath, their bare legs showing as they moved their brightly coloured slippers oddly at variance with the austerity of their sombre habits, as were their red lips and shrewd greedy eyes.

While Moll helped Clarinda take off her clothes, the Abbess chattered away.

"This place isn't anythin' like as fine as Sir Francis Dashwood's Club," she said. "He had a banquetin' 'all and an inner Temple in the very deepest part of the 'ill. There was also a stream filled with what the Brothers called 'unholy water' where the newly initiated members were baptised. It was all on a grand scale, but 'ere we have everythin' lumped together. Not that they spares any expense when it comes to the food and drink."

Clarinda said nothing and Moll continued,

"All brought down from London, it is, and the servants too. Mr. Vernon says they be blindfolded so they won't be knowin' where they're goin'. But if that be true, I bet they had a peep or two so that the knowledge will come in useful one day or another."

"When Clarinda was completely naked, Moll slipped over her head a long white Grecian gown made of thin silk, which Clarinda felt with a sick embarrassment did little to hide her nakedness.

There was a gold ribbon to tie round her waist and Moll released her hair to fall in a flaming silken cloud over her shoulders and down her back and tied a gold ribbon on top of her head.

"Lovely hair you has, dearie," she exclaimed. "I used to be able to sit on mine when I was young, not that it was ever the pretty colour of yours. But that be a long time ago."

"Why do – you do – this?" Clarinda asked, conscious of something wistful and almost human in the woman's voice.

Moll's lips twisted in a wry smile.

"Money! What other reason is there for a woman my age to do such things? The older you get the lower you sink. This is what livin' too long does for a woman who could once attract the most fashionable gentlemen in St. James's."

She gave a wry laugh and then continued,

"'Tis no use gettin' morbid, I've got a few years left yet."

"Just think of the money I could give you," Clarinda said, making a last effort to save herself. "You could live in comfort for the rest of your life and never have to come to places like – this. You could have your own house. You could be comfortable, you could grow old gracefully."

As Moll seemed to hesitate for a moment, Clarinda whispered insistently,

"Is there not one gentleman here who would help me? One who needs money?"

"That's just what I was thinkin' myself," Moll answered. "But you do see, dearie, I don't know who they be. They wear masks because they don't wish to be recognised. I knows Mr. Vernon, of course, because 'e engages me. I know Sir Gerald, 'e's a *habitué* at the bawdy house where I works. But the others I may have met them, but when they're in their robes and wearin' masks they all look so alike. Most of them are too rich to need money, the rest would sooner have the thrill and excitement of bein' 'ere tonight than anythin' you could give them in compensation."

"I – understand," Clarinda said and her voice was dead as if she felt her last vestige of hope had been taken from her.

It seemed to her as if Moll too shrugged away a dream of what might have been.

"You look real pretty," she said. "I can say one thing, there's never been a Venus in the Club who has looked as pretty as you."

"What happens to – them – afterwards?" Clarinda stammered.

"It won't help you to ask questions," Moll replied sharply.

"What questions does she want answering?" a voice enquired from the door and both Moll and Clarinda started as Nicholas came through the curtain.

He looked almost unbelievably frightening, Clarinda thought, wearing a monk's habit of blood red, the hood pulled over his head, his eyes glittering evilly through the mask beneath it.

"Come," he said, "the room is filling up, the banquet is beginning. The Brothers must have a chance to see the beauty of Venus, through whose purity our Master will come to us tonight."

He held out his hand and with an almost superhuman effort Clarinda forced herself to put her cold fingers in his.

She had the impulse to make one more last appeal to him, but in the light of the candles which illuminated the room, she could see that the pupils of his eyes were dilated. Black and dark as jet they stared at her and she knew without being told that Nicholas had taken some sort of drug.

There was no hope of an appeal there, she thought, and in her heart she returned to her prayers.

'*Help me – God – help me,*' she prayed and knew that it was only her prayers that would strengthen her not to scream and not to run away uselessly.

'I must keep clear-headed and preserve my strength to kill myself,' she decided.

Then she was drawn from the robing room into the passage as Nicholas moved forward.

They descended lower into the bowels of the earth and suddenly the great banqueting cave lay before them. It was very large in circumference and almost circular. The walls, like the passages, were draped in red velvet and iron sconces held thick long candles. There were couches round the walls and in small alcoves veiled with curtains.

In the centre of the hall there were tables laid with silver crystal glass and lace-edged damask and there were footmen in powdered wigs and gold-braided livery carrying in dishes, pouring out wine and waiting on the guests who sprawled at the tables, each with a woman at his side.

Already, Clarinda noted, many of the nuns had discarded their habits and thrown away their wimples. Their hair had been freed, which alone, in many cases, was the only cover for their nakedness.

There was a great chatter of voices and the sound of raucous laughter, but when she and Nicholas appeared there was a sudden silence.

Then, the company rose somewhat unsteadily as they processed down the centre of the great cave towards the Altar, which Clarinda saw was set under a high arch engraved with magical signs to the right of the descending passageway.

There was no need for her to see the huge crucifix upside-down, the tall black candles or the white marble slab of the Altar itself, just long and wide enough to hold the naked body of a woman. She had known what to expect!

Then she saw on the centre of six broad steps leading up to the Altar there was a gold chair, a kind of throne, on which she knew she must sit until the Black Mass took place.

Slowly and in silence Nicholas led her to her place.

She tried as she moved not to notice the men's eyes leering through their masks at her nakedness only partially veiled by her white gown. She tried to pray, tried not to think of the inverted crucifix ahead of her and tried to remember that the evil in this place came not from anything supernatural but only from the hearts and minds of those gathered there.

When finally she was seated on the chair prepared for her, Nicholas gave her a mocking bow.

"I congratulate you again, Clarinda, on your self-control," he declared. "You are indeed worthy of the great honour to be accorded you tonight. I see too I am wise in my intention of marrying you after the Master has visited us."

"I have nothing to say to you, Nicholas," she replied and to her relief her voice sounded steady and unafraid. "You know that what you are doing is evil, wicked and a blasphemous offence against God."

She tried to look at him defiantly, but she knew as she heard him laughing that he was unimpressed.

"You will change your mind later," he responded, "and be grateful to me."

The words were inexpressibly horrible in all that they implied.

He left her then and she saw him sitting down at a table where the women seemed more abandoned than at any other and where two of the men already were almost incapably drunk.

Clarinda glanced round the room. She saw there were great braziers on either side of her in which she realised that magical herbs were burning. She could smell them and knew that they were strong narcotics and felt as if already their power was seeping into her senses and making it hard for her to think.

She was aware that the herbs would include belladonna, hemlock, verbena and mandrake and she told herself that she must not lose the clearness of her mind or have the sharpness of her intentions blunted.

Almost immediately in front of her was a table where the occupants were being served with exotic dishes. But what interested Clarinda was the glittering silver that they ate their food with.

She could then see the knives. Sharp, ground to a fine edge and pointed, one would pass straight into her body without any tremendous strength being necessary.

Somehow she must seize one. But she knew that she must wait until the reactions of the men and women using them had become so dulled with drink and the exotic fragrance from the braziers that her action would be too swift for it to be prevented.

'Help me – *please God – help me*,' she prayed yet again.

As the clamour of drunken voices and feminine shrieks now rose higher and higher, she looked no longer at the debauched company below her, but turned her eyes upwards towards the unadorned chalk ceiling.

'I don't want to – look, I don't want to – see,' she thought. 'It is too degrading. It is a – horrid spectacle of men and women who have discarded all the refinements of – civilisation to become lower than – animals.'

She clasped her hands together and said her prayers – prayers she had repeated all her life before she went to bed and prayers she had learnt from her mother when she was only a tiny child. And as the beautiful words of the prayers themselves brought her some solace, she began to pray harder than ever that she would be rescued.

She knew that only Lord Melburne could save her, for no one else knew where she was and no one else would be capable of formulating any plan of getting her away even if they wished to come to her rescue.

'Send him – oh God – send him in time,' she prayed, 'and if not let me die – quickly. Let me die bravely without – screaming and without – crying out with the – pain of it. Help me – please God – help me.'

It seemed to her as if her prayers carried her away in spirit from the debauchery around her and it must have been a long time later that something attracted her attention.

She thought for one moment that the Black Mass itself was just about to start. She had already seen the Priest, the man who had taken Dene's Farm as a tenant, and recognised him as he wore not a monk's robe but a red cassock. Even with a mask there was no mistaking his bald head and the fat folds of his numerous chins.

But the Priest was drinking at a table at the far end of the cave and she saw that various men, having finished dinner, were moving about quarrelling over the women or performing obscene acts.

Some were fighting amongst themselves so that one Brother fell sprawling on the floor and his monk's robe fell back to reveal a wine-soaked shirt and a brilliant diamond cravat pin flashing in the light of the candles.

Then amongst the hubbub and general disorder Clarinda noticed a tall figure staggering drunkenly amongst the tables and coming, it seemed, directly towards her. She noticed he was carrying in his hands several bottles, occasionally lifting one unsteadily to his lips and yet never relinquishing the bottles themselves as if greedily he wished to imbibe more than anyone else.

He tripped against the step immediately in front of her and nervously she shrank back in her chair, afraid that he might fall upon her. As she did so, she heard a voice she knew say very softly,

"Be ready to run."

For a moment she could hardly believe that she was not imagining the words. Then she knew with a sudden leap in her heart that her prayers had been answered.

Lord Melburne was here! He had actually entered the caves and, masked and wearing a red robe, he looked like one of the Brothers.

Having spoken to Clarinda he righted himself and staggered on. Suddenly with a swift movement he flung three of the bottles he carried into the big brazier immediately to the left of the Altar steps.

There was a blinding sheet of flame as the neat spirit took fire and then the bottles began to burst with a noise just like pistol shots and pieces of glass flying out dangerously so that everyone in the vicinity ducked their heads.

At the first sound Lord Melburne turned, seized Clarinda by the hand and, dragging her from her seat on the steps, ran with her towards the entrance. There were two more bottles in his other hand and these he flung into the brazier which they passed on the other side of the Altar.

Again there was that flashing tongue of flame and, as it dazzled those who looked at it, Clarinda found herself being dragged with incredible swiftness up the sloping passageway, which was the only exit from the caves.

She almost fell as her feet were caught in her robe, but, as she gave a little cry, she felt herself picked up in strong arms and Lord Melburne, holding her close against his breast, started running wildly up the carpeted incline.

She could feel his heart beating against hers and knew that because he was so tall he had to keep his head bent, which impeded their progress. But no one stopped them until, as they had almost reached the iron gateway, there was a roaring voice from behind them.

Clarinda heard it only too clearly and felt a sudden agony of fear lest they should be stopped. She remembered the pistol worn by the man who inspected the members at the entrance and knew that, if he should draw it, Lord Melburne could do little to save himself, encumbered as he was with her in his arms.

But the man in the doorway was half-asleep. He then looked up at their approach, saw a masked gentleman and a woman leaving together and made no effort to prevent them until it was too late.

Only as they rushed passed him did he rise slowly to his feet and turn his head towards the shouting man coming behind them. Clarinda could hear Nicholas screaming hysterically as he too pounded up the narrow passageway.

"Stop, *blast you*! Stop them, *you bleeding fools*!" he yelled.

It was dark outside. But by the light of the flares it was easy to see Lord Melburne's carriage drawn up just by the entrance, the footman standing with the door open, the horses moving restlessly.

Lord Melburne literally flung Clarinda onto the back seat and jumped in himself even as the coachman sprung the horses and the footman clambered like a monkey onto the box.

As they moved there were shouts from behind them, two pistol shots echoed deafeningly in the darkness and at least one bullet buried itself in the back of the carriage

There was more outcry in which could be heard Nicholas's voice yelling out abuse and shouting obscenities. Then there was a scream, high and shrill, a scream like that of an animal in pain, before the horses, gathering speed, swept them out of earshot and Clarinda knew that she was safe.

For a moment she could hardly believe it was true. The horror of what she had passed through still gripped her so she felt that she must still be dreaming.

She was safe, she told herself – safe from being defiled or from having to take her own life and safe from a degradation so revolting that she dare not think about it.

She was safe – safe – *safe*.

But, as she drew a deep breath to thank her rescuer, her self-control broke. Tears that she had kept in check for the whole evening swept over her like a tempest and, without knowing what she did, she threw herself against Lord Melburne and hid her face in his shoulder.

He pulled off his mask, shrugged himself out of the red robes and he put his arms round her.

Racked by agonising tears that shook her whole body, she was trembling from head to foot.

He held her closer still. Then, realising how cold she was, not only from her nakedness but also from fear and misery, he picked up a rug from the floor and drew it closely round her.

She was past knowing what he did or what happened, she could only sob with a violence which seemed to tear her whole body apart.

"It's all right," he said gently, "you are safe. Don't cry, Clarinda, no one shall touch you and no one shall hurt you now. You are safe."

She could not answer him, but could only sob blindly and helplessly until his coat was wet with her tears.

He knew that there was nothing he could do for the moment except give her the comfort of his arms. He could not have believed that a woman could weep so desperately or tremble so helplessly against him.

At length, as the carriage was nearing The Priory, she stammered in a voice thick with tears,

"You came – I prayed – and p-prayed – but I did not think – God w-would be able – to s-send you."

"But He *did* send me," Lord Melburne answered gently, "and you now need no longer be afraid, Clarinda."

He felt her little hands clutch the lapels of his coat.

"Nicholas!" she gasped. "He will come after – me, he will – follow us – he will kill – you."

"Don't be afraid, I have saved you, Clarinda, and I will protect you. Are you listening to me? And I will protect you from Nicholas and from everyone else. He shall never touch you again."

"You don't – understand," she cried, "he is – e-evil, he is – wicked – he believes in the – powers of d-darkness, he thinks he can evoke the Devil – he will k-kill you to get – me back."

"You have to trust me," Lord Melburne said. "I swear to you, Clarinda, that you need no longer be afraid."

Even as he spoke, he knew that she was too distraught to be soothed by his words as the terror she had experienced was too deeply engrained in her. He could feel her still trembling in his arms like a wild bird caught in a trap.

"Clarinda, trust me, I swear to you that nothing more will happen," he insisted.

"Y-you don't – understand," she murmured and now she was weeping again, no longer with relief but with a new terror that was more real than anything else she had experienced the whole evening.

The carriage came to a stop at the front door of The Priory and Lord Melburne, holding Clarinda close in his arms, stepped out.

He carried her into the hall, Betty was waiting and so was old Bates, both white-faced and agitated.

"Miss Clarinda is all right," Lord Melburne told them in a quiet voice, "but she has been badly frightened. I will take her upstairs."

He carried her up to her bedroom, Betty going ahead to open the door.

He laid her gently down on the pillows, but Clarinda still clung to him.

"He is coming – a-after me – I k-know it," she moaned. "Don't – leave me – please don't – 1-leave me."

Very gently Lord Melburne disengaged her fingers from his coat and, putting his hand under her chin, he turned her face up towards his.

"Listen," he said, "listen to me carefully, Clarinda. I am going to leave you now for a very short time. There will be men here to guard you and they will kill anyone who dares to approach you. Do you follow me? Nicholas will never come near you again, that I promise."

"He will – k-kill – y-you," Clarinda whispered.

"No, *I* shall kill *him*," Lord Melburne replied deliberately.

His words arrested her and she stared at him wide-eyed. For a moment her tears stopped.

"You have been so brave," he said quietly, "and so magnificently courageous. Don't give way now, just trust me,"

She lay very still, looking up into his face. She could see him clearly in the candlelight, his chin squared, his mouth grim and his eyes hard and determined.

Then she stammered almost beneath her breath,

"You – are – s-sure?"

"Quite sure," he answered.

She put out her hands again as if she would prevent him from leaving her, but he turned to Betty.

"You will stay here all night with your Mistress. Lock the door and put some furniture in front of it. You will be protected, but I wish to take every precaution. Do you understand?"

"Yes, my Lord," Betty replied.

"Don't – g-go – I beg of you not to – go," Clarinda pleaded.

He moved back to lay his hand on hers.

"You know I must do what is right, no one knows that better than you."

Then he had left the room and she heard the key turning in the lock behind him.

"Bates, can you handle a gun?"

"I was in the Army for five years, my Lord,"

"And so was the footman on my box. Show me where your Master keeps his firearms."

He walked to the front door as he spoke.

"James," he called, "I want you."

The footman came hurrying into the house and Lord Melburne let Bates lead him to a small room which, opening off the hall, contained every weapon appertaining to sport. Lord Melburne picked up a fowling piece and a musket, handed one to Bates and the other to the footman,

"Load these," he said. "Stand at the top of the stairs outside Miss Clarinda's room and shoot anybody, with the exception of myself, who dares come into the house. Don't argue, don't hesitate, just shoot and be accurate."

"Very good, my Lord," the two men said almost simultaneously.

Lord Melburne opened a box in which lay Sir Roderick's duelling pistols. He took out one, loaded it and then said to James,

"Put this box in the coach."

"You are going back, my Lord?" Bates asked.

"I am going back," Lord Melburne answered grimly and, without saying anything more, he went down the steps and re-entered his carriage.

CHAPTER SEVEN

There was the sound of birds singing and the soft buzz of a bee against the windowpanes. Clarinda lay listening for a little while before she opened her eyes.

The sun coming in from the big casement facing her was almost blinding and she stared about her in bewilderment at the carved posts of the great bed she was in, at the blue draped curtains, the gilt mirrors and gold framed pictures.

"Where am I?" she asked aloud.

In an instant Betty was beside her.

"Oh, Miss Clarinda, you're awake!" she exclaimed.

"Yes, I am awake," Clarinda answered slowly. "I seem to have slept for a long time."

"Five days, miss," Betty told her.

"Five days!"

Clarinda felt almost speechless.

"But why? And where am I?"

"You're at Melburne, miss. His Lordship felt it best to bring you here in case when you was well again you felt frightened."

"Then I have been ill?" Clarinda asked.

Betty shook her head.

"No, miss, only sufferin' from shock, is what the physician said. You cried and cried and he gave you a sleepin' draught. Then he thought, or maybe it was his Lordship, 'twould be best for you not to know what was happenin' till it were all over."

Clarinda raised herself on her pillow.

"What was all over?" she asked.

"The funeral, miss."

"Then Uncle Roderick is dead!" Clarinda cried. "I ought to have been there, I ought to have been with him!"

"Now, miss, you're not to upset yourself," Betty replied. "The Master died peaceful-like the followin' afternoon after his Lordship saved you. He didn't know what had happened, no one told him and his Lordship has seen to everythin'."

"When was he buried?" Clarinda asked in a low voice.

"Yesterday afternoon, miss, and Mr. Nicholas with him."

Clarinda sat bolt upright, her eyes wide.

"Nicholas is – dead too!"

She cried the words aloud.

"Did his Lordship – ?"

"No, no," Betty interrupted quickly.

"'Twas not his Lordship who killed Mr. Nicholas, 'twas Simple Sarah."

"Simple Sarah?"

Clarinda stared at her maid in astonishment.

"Yes, miss, she killed Mr. Nicholas as I understands, when he came from the cave. She was a-waitin' for him hidden behind the yew trees. She drove a knife into his back not once but half a dozen times."

"So Nicholas is dead," Clarinda sighed in a low voice.

"His Lordship'll want to tell you about it himself, miss," Betty remarked firmly. "The doctor said that if you woke you could get up today. And it'll be better for you to walk about after all the sleepin' draughts you've had. I'll go fetch your breakfast, miss. You'll feel quite yourself when you've had somethin' to eat."

Betty went from the room and Clarinda stared blindly at the sunshine.

So Nicholas was dead! She could hardly believe it.

Now the terror she had suffered in the caves came flooding back into her memory. She had been saved, saved by a huge miracle it seemed and she could not conceive how Lord Melburne could have done it.

She could hear the noise of the exploding wine bottles, she could feel him gripping her arm and pulling her away from the Altar, she could remember that frightening rush towards the entrance and she could hear Nicholas shouting behind them and finally when they were safe in the carriage the explosion of the pistol shots echoing after them.

Clarinda put her hands up to her eyes. Could she ever forget the terror of those hours when she had known that, if Lord Melburne did not come, she must somehow contrive to kill herself?

And yet he had saved her, the man who she had hated, the man who for four years she had thought of with bitter contempt. She would have to thank him, she thought, she would have to tell him how grateful she was.

And she wondered how she could ever find the words.

Then she remembered how she had cried in his arms and she felt ashamed that he should have seen her so weak and so helpless. If only she had managed to keep her self-control until she had reached home. She remembered that she had pleaded with him to stay with her and felt herself blush at the memory.

When Betty had dressed her and arranged her hair elegantly, Clarinda turned resolutely towards the stairs, even though her heart was pounding unaccountably and she felt shyer and more embarrassed than she had ever felt before.

She had never imagined a house could be so magnificent. The great carved staircase was impressive enough, but there were high gilt mirrors over carved gold tables, family portraits and huge crystal chandeliers to admire besides the exquisite colouring of the walls. She was to learn later that much of the furniture had been designed especially for Melburne by the Adam brothers.

The burnished gold of the sofas and the fireside stools seemed to vie in brilliance with exquisitely carved sconces on pale green walls, which made a perfect setting for a collection of pictures that Clarinda had always heard spoken of as being unsurpassed.

Much as she longed to linger and admire Lord Melburne's possessions, she knew that she must first find him, even though for some unaccountable reason she could not explain to herself she felt afraid of seeing him again.

As a footman opened the library door for her, she had the impression of walls lined with books, of a room so beautifully proportioned that for a moment she could only gasp at what she saw.

Then she was aware that standing by the mantelpiece was the tall, elegant figure of the man who never failed to make her feel small and insignificant

He was exquisitely dressed as usual and inevitably she felt ashamed of the shabbiness of her gown. All that she was intending to say seemed to disappear from her mind.

Tongue-tied she could only look at him with large eyes, having no idea that the sunshine glinting on the fiery gold of her hair made her look like a very small Goddess who had just descended from Mount Olympus.

"You are better?"

She had forgotten how deep his voice was and how penetrating his grey eyes. It seemed to her he observed every detail of her appearance, the paleness of her cheeks, the fragility of her face, which was a little thinner than when he last saw it, the agitation of her heart and the sudden trembling of her hands.

"I am quite —well," Clarinda murmured in reply.

He held out his hand towards her.

"Do come and sit down," he suggested and, as his tone was kind for some extraordinary reason she felt at that moment near to tears.

'It is those horrible sleeping draughts, they have made me weak,' she told herself.

She then forced herself to walk towards him and seat herself on the edge of the sofa. She looked up at him, thinking how tall he was and even the vast proportions of the room could not dwarf him.

"Were you surprised to find yourself at Melburne?" he asked unexpectedly,

"I was astonished," Clarinda answered. "How did you get me here?"

"You are not a very heavy object to move," he answered with a smile. "You were well wrapped up in blankets so you suffered no ill-effects."

"I understand from my maid that you thought I would feel safer here than at The Priory."

"That is so."

Then, as though the question burst from her lips and she could refrain no longer from asking it, she enquired slowly,

"How did you manage to save me? Even now I can hardly believe that my prayers were answered."

"You prayed that I would come?" he asked in a low voice.

"I prayed as I have never prayed before that God would send you," she told him, "and that you would find some way of escape for me from those monsters."

"What happened was in direct answer to your prayers for I assure you that when I heard where you had gone, I could not imagine how I could contrive to enter the caves, not being a member of the Club."

Clarinda clasped her hands together.

"I thought of that too," she said, "but somehow, I don't know why, I felt you would find a way. If you had not – "

She paused.

"What if I had not managed it?" Lord Melburne questioned.

"I intended to kill myself," she answered simply. "I knew how to do it and it would not have been hard to get hold of a knife."

He sat down beside her.

"I want you to forget what happened that evening," he said and his voice was grave. "It is something no woman should have had to endure, yet I want to tell you that, when I saw you with your face turned up towards the ceiling, I could hardly believe that anyone, anyone in the world, could have been as brave as you were."

There was something in his voice that made her feel even shyer than she had felt before. The colour flooded into her face and she looked away from him.

"I tried not to look at what was happening around me," she answered, "but just to pray."

"That is what I felt you must be doing," he said.

"But how – how did you get in?" Clarinda asked. "I must – know,"

"It is a question I had asked myself a hundred times before I found the answer," Lord Melburne admitted, "as I stood outside the caves watching the guests arriving. Then when I saw them adjusting masks before they entered, I knew that was the answer to my question."

"I don't understand."

"I waited," he continued, "until I recognised the Coat of Arms on one of the coaches. It belonged, I knew, to a young Nobleman who is heavily in debt, a stupid young man who has wasted his heritage gambling and taking part in mad adventures, every one of which has cost him money. I drew him on one side and I offered him quite a large sum of money if he would give me his mask and his token of membership,"

"And he agreed?" Clarinda asked breathlessly.

"He needed a little persuasion," Lord Melburne replied with a twist of his lips.

"You mean you forced him to give you what you wanted?"

"I think by the time he reached London and, when he received the money the following morning, he was grateful to me," Lord Melburne answered. "The evening was spoilt anyway for them after I had spirited you away."

"You were clever – very clever," Clarinda said.

"Perhaps it was all your prayers that helped me once again," Lord Melburne suggested. "For I promise you that as I walked down into the cave and saw you sitting there, I had not the slightest idea of how, with at least a hundred men to contend with, I could possibly save you."

"And then you thought of the wine in the bottles."

"Brandy, the best brandy!" Lord Melburne corrected her with a smile. "It burns well and the bursting bottles would, I just knew, divert the attention of those who were already half-stupefied by the excessive amount they had drunk."

"Supposing someone had penetrated your disguise?" Clarinda asked him breathlessly.

"Then I should have been in trouble. But it did not happen."

"And then after you had left me at The Priory, when you went back – what happened?"

"I had intended to challenge Nicholas Vernon to a duel," Lord Melburne replied and his voice was grim. "If he had not been gentleman enough to accept it, then I would have shot him down as I would shoot down a mad dog. But I was too late."

"Betty told me that Simple Sarah – had killed him," Clarinda said.

"It must have been his scream we heard as we drove away," Lord Melburne reflected. "When I got back, the last of the guests were tearing back to London, frightened of a scandal and terrified of being involved in the enquiries that they felt must be inevitable."

"Only Nicholas was there?" Clarinda asked.

"He was on the point of death," Lord Melburne said, "and because I was afraid that you might be involved in any enquiries that might be made, I had him put in my carriage and I took him back to The Priory."

"You took him to The Priory?" Clarinda echoed in horror. "But how could you?"

"It was his home," Lord Melburne replied. "Your uncle's physician attended to him, but there was nothing anyone could do. He died an hour after his arrival."

His Lordship paused and then continued,

"That prevented there being any investigations of the evening's proceedings. I swore that I had found him stabbed in The Priory drive. And that is why what happened that terrible evening, as far as you are concerned, Clarinda, is best forgotten."

She did not answer him and after a moment he urged her gently,

"Try and forget. No good can come if you torture yourself now it is all over. Forget it as if it was a nightmare of no evil consequence save that you were frightened."

"I will try," she whispered. Then with an effort she raised her face to his. "But first, my Lord, I must thank you."

He rose from her side.

"I have no wish for your thanks. It will only embarrass me and indeed I have reproached myself bitterly that I did not anticipate you might be involved in circumstances so bestial."

"And why should you have anticipated it?" Clarinda asked bewildered.

"Because I had heard about the caves and the meetings of the Hell Fire Club that were being held there, because I realised you were right and the man at Dene's Farm was a Priest, and because I was such a fool not to

~141~

realise at once that Nicholas Vernon would never forgive you for taking away his inheritance."

Lord Melburne spoke with an angry voice.

Then he said sharply,

"But this is all to be forgotten as well. You will not speak of it again, Clarinda, do you understand, either to me or to the servants. They have all been warned that if they repeat to anyone what happened that night, they will be dismissed without a character reference."

"I understand," Clarinda said quietly. "So you have saved not only me but the honour of the Vernons."

"I have done my best," Lord Melburne reflected.

"And Simple Sarah, what has happened to her?" Clarinda enquired.

"She drowned herself," Lord Melburne replied. "And that means there will be no trial and again it closes a chapter, a chapter that must never be reopened."

Clarinda gave a deep sigh as if it came from the very depths of her being.

"Thank you, my Lord," she said. "I promise you that I am deeply and sincerely grateful."

"And now I want to talk to you about something very different," Lord Melburne told her. "Do you feel well enough to listen?"

"Of course," she answered. "I am completely recovered. I can quite understand why you wished me to be unconscious these last few days, but it was unnecessary. But I should have been brave enough to attend my uncle's funeral."

"It was an ordeal that I did not wish you to be subjected to," Lord Melburne said.

There was something proprietary in his tone, which made Clarinda raise her eyes quickly to his.

"Uncle Roderick's will has been read?" she asked.

"Yes," Lord Melburne answered. "He has left, as indeed you well know, everything that he possessed, The Priory and his very considerable fortune to you, Clarinda. You are now a very wealthy and very enviable young woman."

Clarinda rose from the sofa and walked across to the window. She stood looking out over the lake before she said,

"I never wanted all that money. I intended to give most of it back to Nicholas, keeping just enough for Betty and myself to have a small house on the estate. I thought we could live there quietly."

"I am afraid that is now impossible," Lord Melburne interposed.

"Not really," she answered. "I can give the money away and you can have the estate. It marches with yours and you will administer it far better than I should do. It was what Uncle Roderick wanted anyway."

"Do you really think that I could accept such a valuable present?" Lord Melburne asked. "No, Clarinda, I have very different plans for you."

She turned round to look at him.

"You have plans for me?" she asked. "I think, my Lord, you have forgotten that now my uncle is dead the arrangement was that you would be free – free to return to your amusements in London. When I asked for your help I was not expecting that you would find yourself involved in such a terrifying situation. I am grateful, more grateful than I can ever say for what you have done, but it is finished. Thank you, but now we can say 'goodbye'."

"May I ask you what you intend to do?" Lord Melburne enquired.

"I will live at The Priory for the moment," Clarinda answered.

"*Alone*?"

The word sounded almost like a pistol shot.

"Betty will be with me and the other servants are here."

"You know as well as I do," Lord Melburne said harshly, "that you cannot live at The Priory unchaperoned. You are not only wealthy, Clarinda, you are also a very beautiful young woman. Surely you can understand that both of those attributes carry their own penalties."

"That is ridiculous," Clarinda countered hotly.

Then she met Lord Melburne's eyes and the words died on her lips.

"I will find myself a chaperone," she said almost submissively.

"Have you anyone in mind?"

"No," she admitted.

"Very well, until someone suitable can be procured, I have another suggestion to make."

"What is that?" Clarinda asked.

"That you should come to London," he answered. "I have already made arrangements for my maternal grandmother, the Dowager Marchioness of Slade, to chaperone you at Melburne House. In your new condition you must take your place in Society. You will,

Clarinda, have a chance to see more of the world than you have seen these past years."

"I think you must be crazed!" Clarinda expostulated. "Do you really credit that you can arrange my life for me, that I would accept the chaperonage of your grandmother or indeed do anything else that you suggest?"

"I was rather expecting that this might be your attitude," Lord Melburne said in his most uncompromising voice. "But I am afraid, Clarinda, you have no choice in the matter."

"I have – no – choice?"

The words seemed to be squeezed from her in her astonishment.

"No," he answered. "Our betrothal, which enabled Sir Roderick to die happy believing that his estate was safe, is I grant you, terminated. But your uncle made another proviso in his will and I admit it was on my suggestion, that until you came of age or married, I should be your Guardian."

For a moment Clarinda was too stupefied to answer him.

Then stammering in her anger she exclaimed,

"Y-you made Uncle Roderick – appoint you – my G-Guardian? How could you do such – a thing, how could you – interfere, how could you – h-humiliate me by assuming such a – position?"

"It is a position," Lord Melburne said sternly, "that I am prepared to relinquish at any moment, Clarinda, either to your husband or to someone I consider would be an adequate or perhaps better Guardian than myself. You have but to name such a person and I will resign at once in his favour. Have you anyone to suggest?"

Clarinda turned away petulantly to stare once again out of the window.

"I know of no one," she said crossly, "but I do *not* want – you."

"That is very obvious," Lord Melburne said, "and I assure you, Clarinda, it is not a duty I would undertake if I did not feel it was imperative that you should be properly looked after."

"Only because I am rich," Clarinda snapped. "When I was poor, no one worried about me in any way."

"On the contrary, I have found you quite a considerable worry ever since I have known you," Lord Melburne replied.

There was a hint of laughter in his voice and Clarinda felt herself blush.

"That was rude and – ungrateful of – me, my Lord," she said shyly. "Please – will you consider – those words – unsaid?"

"Certainly," Lord Melburne replied, "as long as you listen to the plans I have made. I am afraid, Clarinda, that much as you may dislike me, you have no alternative at the moment but to accept them."

Almost as though he compelled her to, Clarinda came from the window to sit down once again on the sofa.

"I am taking you to London," Lord Melburne explained, "because I consider it is in your best interest that your horizon should be widened, that you should meet girls of your own age and gentlemen who will undoubtedly find you very attractive."

There was something dry and a little sarcastic about his voice that made Clarinda glance at him sharply.

"My grandmother will help you buy the right sort of clothes in which you can make your debut into the fashionable world."

"Surely I am in mourning for Uncle Roderick?" Clarinda interrupted.

"That is also provided for in your uncle's will. He specially requested that no one should wear black for him nor should there be any period of mourning whatsoever."

"That is your doing!" Clarinda exclaimed. "You knew if I was in mourning I could not go to London."

"On the contrary, I believe that your uncle inserted that particular clause because he was thinking of the expense."

Once again because she had been rude, Clarinda felt the blood rising in her cheeks.

"You will, I think," Lord Melburne continued, "find the Social world very different from your present conception of it."

"I doubt it," Clarinda said hotly. "I have now met you and I have met Nicholas, two gentlemen of fashion who have not endeared the *Beau Ton* to me, if that is the right term for the Society that you move in."

She paused as if she expected him to speak.

When he said nothing, she continued,

"I know that as a woman I should be really looking forward to attending balls, masques and assemblies. But I do not want to meet the people who enjoy such entertainments. I want to stay here in the country, where I shall not be out of place, where gentlemen like your Lordship will not make me feel uncomfortable because my gown is unsmart and my hair not dressed in the latest fashion."

Again, she seemed to wait for his comment before she went on,

"I want to live quietly without always feeling intimidated that I shall do the wrong thing or having to make polite conversation to people with whom I have not the slightest interest in common,"

She spoke hotly, her hands clenched together in her intensity.

Then she realised that Lord Melburne was quite unmoved by her protest.

"If after several months in London, you tell me the same thing," he said quietly, "then we can readjust your plans for the future."

"You think you can do what you like with me, do you not?" she said furiously. "Have I no say in anything? After all it is my money that is going to pay for all this nonsense."

"Then let us hope that your money will teach you to behave more like a sensible woman than a hysterical schoolgirl," Lord Melburne replied.

She felt as if he had hit her and, because he had aroused an almost blind anger in her, she stormed,

"I hate you, do you understand? I would rather have anyone – *anyone* as my Guardian than you! *I hate you*, I despise you! I shall never forget and never forgive what you did to my friend."

"To your friend?" Lord Melburne asked.

There was a sudden glint in his eyes as if he realised that he was needling her into telling him what he had long wanted to know.

"Yes, to my friend – Jessica Tansley," Clarinda cried. "And now can you tell me that I should not be afraid of coming to London to meet fashionable gentlemen like yourself!"

"Jessica Tansley," Lord Melburne repeated. "It is strange, but I cannot for the life of me remember ever hearing that name before."

"How can you say such a thing?" Clarinda raged. "How can you utter such a falsehood or try to deceive me! You are impossible, utterly and completely impossible and that is why I hate you."

She turned as she spoke and ran from the room, determined as she went that he should not see the tears in her eyes, tears of weakness and of rage combined.

Lord Melburne stood for a long time when she had left him repeating almost beneath his breath the name 'Jessica Tansley'.

Then speaking aloud he said,

"I swear I have never heard of the woman."

Upstairs Clarinda wept in her bedroom for some minutes before resolutely she wiped her eyes and sent for Betty.

"Oh, miss," Betty cried, as she came into the room. "Has his Lordship told you we're leavin' for London this very afternoon? 'Tis the most excitin' thing I've ever known. Are you not thrilled, Miss Clarinda?"

"No, I am not," Clarinda answered crossly. "I want to stay here, Betty, in the country."

"Oh, but Miss Clarinda, you'd feel real sad and gloomy at The Priory. There seemed a shadow over the whole place before we came away. What with the Master and Mr. Nicholas a-dyin' it gives me a sort of creepy feelin', it does really. I wants to see London. And his Lordship's valet has promised he'll take me out one evenin' and show me the sights."

"Have you packed?" Clarinda asked.

"There's not much to pack, Miss Clarinda," Betty answered frankly. "And Mrs. Foster, the lady who's been chaperonin' you since you've been here, says there's no point in takin' a lot of things with us since his Lordship's grandmother will want to buy everythin' new. Her Ladyship is old, but they tells me she's a great personality and of tremendous importance wherever she goes."

"I am frightened – I am frightened, Betty," Clarinda exclaimed.

"Now, Miss Clarinda, you've never been feared of anythin'. Why, Sir Roderick has said over and over again that there's never been anyone who'd take a high fence like you."

"I can face things I understand," Clarinda answered, "but it's not like entering a new world where everything is so strange and where I shall make mistakes at every turn."

"No you'll not, not with her Ladyship there to look after you," Betty said. "Besides, Miss Clarinda, they all say at Melburne you're the prettiest young lady they've ever seen. What's the point of hidin' your face in the country with only a lot of turnip-tops to see it? You can do that when you're old and ugly."

Clarinda laughed suddenly.

"Are you thinking of me or yourself, Betty?"

"I'm thinkin' of both of us, if I tells the truth, miss," Betty replied. "I'm not as young as I was and this may be my last chance to go anywhere and meet anyone. Why,

~150~

do you know, there are over thirty menservants in this house? Thirty, miss! It gives a woman a real choice."

Clarinda laughed again.

"Perhaps I am being silly, Betty, It is just that I don't want to do what his Lordship wants me to."

"Not after he saved you, miss?" Betty said. "That seems a mite ungrateful! His Lordship was so wonderful that night, he was really. He told me to stay with you all night. He set old Bates and his own footman outside your door with guns and told them to shoot anyone who came into the house. They would have too!"

Betty's eyes glistened as if she would have enjoyed the bloodshed.

"Then when Sir Roderick died the next day," she continued, "there'd have been a real muddle if His Lordship had not been in charge here. Just like a General, he was, commandin' everyone to do this and do that. I swear, Miss Clarinda, you would have felt proud if you'd been here to see how everythin' was arranged with no fuss and no complaints."

Clarinda said nothing and after a minute Betty went on,

"'Tis not like you, miss, to be ungrateful and ungracious."

"And I am both to Lord Melburne," Clarinda agreed. "Betty, why does he upset me so much?"

"I think it's because you've not seen many gentlemen," Betty said, "only Mr. Nicholas, and he doesn't count and, of course, Mr. Wilsdon, who was much too young. When you get to London, miss, you'll be a big success, you see if you're not."

"I don't want to be a success," Clarinda said, but her words did not sound convincing even to herself.

They set off immediately after luncheon. Clarinda found she was journeying to London in his Lordship's travelling carriage. It was light and well-sprung, but it was closed and she had hoped that Lord Melburne might ask her to drive with him in his high perch phaeton. But perhaps because she had been so rude and disagreeable he did not invite her to accompany him and rather forlornly she stepped into the carriage by herself.

They had eaten a light meal in the oval dining room, but Major Foster and his wife were also present and Clarinda had no chance of speaking alone with Lord Melburne. She knew that she ought to apologise and she wanted to ask him questions about his grandmother, but there was no opportunity.

Bending forward to wave 'goodbye' to the Fosters, she had her last glimpse of Melburne, and she was conscious that Lord Melburne in his phaeton was already speeding ahead up the drive.

"He might have taken me with him," she sighed, but admitted ruefully that it was her own fault that he had no desire for her company.

She would have been surprised if she had known that the Dowager Marchioness of Slade was giving her grandson a berating to the same effect when he arrived at Melburne House in Berkeley Square at least thirty minutes ahead of Clarinda.

"You don't mean to say, Buck, that you let the poor child travel to London alone?" the Dowager enquired, sitting bolt upright with her shoulders back and her head held high.

She looked an extremely formidable old lady until an acute beholder noticed the twinkle in her eye and realised that she had an irresistible humour that made her grandson laugh and a shrewdness that kept the female part of her relatives permanently in apprehension of what she might uncover next.

"Clarinda is, as it so happens," Lord Melburne answered, "somewhat incensed with me and I really could not contemplate two hours of argument as to why she should not come to London."

"She has no wish to come?" the Dowager enquired in some surprise.

"No, indeed," Lord Melburne replied. "She has a vast dislike of the fashionable world, having never seen it and knowing nothing about it."

"Is she bird-witted?" the Dowager hazarded.

"I don't think so," Lord Melburne answered. "She has run The Priory Estate, which as you know, Grandmama, is very large, almost single-handed for the last year and Foster tells me that everything is in the most excellent order. She has kept the accounts, which shows, if nothing else, that she has a head for mathematics."

"Don't tell me she is that really terrifying thing, a female with a brainbox!" the Dowager quizzed him. "I swear to you, Buck, if you have inflicted some plain-faced intellectual upon me, I will walk out of this house tonight."

"You will not find Clarinda plain," Lord Melburne replied. "She is quite one of the most beautiful creatures I have ever seen. She is so unsophisticated. She has more courage than I believed it possible for any woman to have and she has an unremitting hatred of me."

"Are you speaking the truth?" the Dowager asked in astonishment. "Are you seriously telling me, Buck, that there is a girl, any girl, anywhere, who does not find you irresistible?"

"Wait till you meet Clarinda," Lord Melburne proposed with a smile.

"Then why," she enquired, "why in Heaven's name are you playing wet nurse to this wench if she has no interest in you and presumably you have none in her?"

"Shall we put it down to a sense of duty, Grandmama? Something that you have always accused me of lacking!"

"I must say there are times, Buck, when you astonish me," the Dowager declared.

"I am glad," her grandson said affectionately, "because I assure you, Grandmama, you are always a surprise to me. No one but you could have responded so quickly to my call for help and no one but you would have come here not knowing what to expect but ready for any adventure that I might involve you in."

"I cannot think why that surprises you," his grandmother snapped at him. "I assure you life is dull enough in Kent listening to people talking incessantly about cherry trees and your Aunt Matilda continually complaining that she is suffering from asthma. There is one thing I could never abide and that is sick females."

"I can think of other things as well," Lord Melburne smiled. "Now that Melburne House is at your disposal, Grandmama, will you give a ball for Clarinda?"

"I will have a look at the girl first," his grandmother replied cautiously. "I am not going to propel an unattractive creature about, not if you go down to me on your knees, Buck, and that is a promise."

"I can assure you there will be no reason for me to fall on my knees," he said. "And incidentally, as I have already told you, Clarinda is indeed a very wealthy young woman and that should make your task much easier,"

"Which means we shall have all the fortune-seekers in London besieging the house," I deplore and despise those slimy creatures who want to marry a woman for her wealth."

"I am sure that you will be able to keep them at bay," Lord Melburne chuckled.

"I thought that was your job as Guardian," the Dowager snapped. "You don't blind me. Buck! You know as well as I do that you have no intention of accepting a neighbour sitting on your boundaries who you don't approve of."

"Grandmama, you are too sharp to be anything but dangerous. I will be honest with you and admit that such a thought had crossed my mind."

"I suppose you would not consider marrying the girl yourself?" the Dowager asked with a sly glance at him. "I have thought for a long time that it would do you good to settle down. And that black-haired minx, Lady Romayne Ramsey, who calls herself your cousin, has the same idea."

"Does nothing escape you, Grandmama?" Lord Melburne asked with a smile. "I assure you that after the way Clarinda raged at me for daring to propose I should be her Guardian, I would be far too scared, even if I wished it, to suggest any other relationship."

"Well, there is one thing that I am sure of," the Dowager said positively. "If this green chit can withstand your much-vaunted attractions, if she has no interest in getting her claws into you like all those other vacant-faced creatures who chase after you like a flock of sheep, then she must be an exceptional girl."

"Quite exceptional, as you will see, for yourself," Lord Melburne answered as the door opened and the butler announced in stentorian tones,

"Miss Clarinda Vernon, my Lord,"

CHAPTER EIGHT

"You are certainly a success!" the Dowager Marchioness observed as she and Clarinda entered the hall of Melburne House and saw the profusion of flowers that awaited them.

There were bouquets and baskets of flowers on every table and arranged along the sides of the marble floor. Their fragrance scented the air and the cards attached to the offerings appeared each to bear a coronet.

"They are indeed lovely," Clarinda exclaimed. "At the same time I feel that they are a tribute not to me but to you, ma'am, and your grandson."

The Dowager smiled.

"I repeat, you are a great success. You enjoyed the ball last night?"

"It was wonderful," Clarinda answered. "I never thought that anything so magnificent would be given for me. I would indeed be ungrateful if I had not enjoyed every moment of it."

The Dowager turned towards the staircase.

"I shall lie down and it would be wise if you took a rest as well, Clarinda, remember tonight we are dining at Carlton House!"

"I have not forgotten," Clarinda replied. "But, although we went to bed so late last night, I am not at all tired. I admit that I was unconscionably late in rising."

"You are becoming fashionable," the Dowager said. "You are perceiving it is quite easy to forget country ways in a short time."

"I am beginning to find that," Clarinda admitted with a smile.

They moved slowly up the stairway because the Dowager's rheumaticky leg prevented her from moving quickly. She paused on the landing.

She then asked Clarinda,

"How many offers did you receive last night?"

"Only two," Clarinda replied, "and both of them from men who I am convinced were more interested in my fortune than in me."

"I think I can guess who they were," the Dowager told her. "What did you say to them?"

"I have an almost routine speech by now. I tell them how much I am honoured by their proposal and suggest they call on my Guardian."

She gave a little laugh,

"I know that his Lordship will deal most firmly with them."

"That is what a Guardian is for," the Dowager agreed, "and in this respect you have kept my grandson exceedingly busy these past weeks. I am told that Mr. Frederick Harley besieges him daily for a more lenient attitude towards his suit."

"He is a horrible little man!" Clarinda exclaimed. "How dare he think that I could ever consider him as a husband."

"Men of marriageable age have a conceit all of their own," the Dowager said, "but tell me, what did the Duke of Kingston say to you last night?"

"He did not offer for me, if that is what you mean. I danced with His Grace twice – or was it three times – and found he had a high opinion of himself."

"With some reason," the Dowager remarked, continuing her way up the stairs.

"Why?" Clarinda enquired.

"His Grace is, without exception, the greatest matrimonial catch in the country," the Dowager explained. "His mother was a Royal Princess, which gives him a special standing not only at Buckingham Palace but in every Court in Europe. Besides this, the Duke is the largest landowner in England. He owns a dozen magnificent houses and he is not unpleasing to look at."

"He is very large and rather overbearing," Clarinda commented in a small voice.

"If he should offer for you, what a triumph it would be," the Dowager ruminated. "Of course, child, I cannot hold out much hope of it. Every ambitious Mama has angled after the Duke since he left Eton and yet at thirty-five he is still a bachelor!"

"Perhaps he is waiting to fall in love," Clarinda suggested.

The Dowager laughed.

"He is far more likely to be waiting for a suitable Princess," she answered. "As you say, the Duke has a very good opinion of himself. At the same time I should like to bring him to your feet just to see the expression of envy, hatred and malice on the face of every woman in Society with a marriageable daughter."

"I don't think they need perturb themselves," Clarinda smiled, "I am quite certain that the Duke was only being polite last night in asking me to dance."

"Perhaps you are being over-modest," the Dowager remarked drily. "There was no one present who did not claim that you were the loveliest *debutante* not only of this Season but of any other."

"That is only because you gave me such a beautiful gown," Clarinda said. "If they had seen me in the old clothes I had to wear at home, they would not have been so enthusiastic."

The Dowager said nothing until they reached the top of the staircase and then she looked at the girl beside her with appraising eyes.

Dressed in the height of fashion, her muslin gown clinging tightly to her slim body, the blue satin ribbons that cupped her small breasts being echoed by the ribbons and feathers in her high-crowned bonnet, Clarinda was almost unbelievably lovely.

"Did you think," she asked in a low voice, not looking straight at the Dowager, "that his Lordship enjoyed the ball?"

"I thought my grandson played his part as host most ably," the Dowager replied. "Did he not congratulate you on your appearance?"

She looked at Clarinda with her shrewd eyes as she spoke and noticed the slight flush which coloured her cheeks.

"His Lordship did say something conventionally complimentary while he was waiting to receive the guests," she admitted, "but he did not ask me to dance."

"I have always been told that my grandson has a rooted objection to prancing about the dance floor," the Dowager said.

"He danced with Lady Romayne," Clarinda replied.

"If he did, I am sure it was none of his seeking," the Dowager exclaimed. "If there was ever a pushing demanding creature, it is that pretentious over-acclaimed female! In my day ladies waited to be chased, they did not make a man feel like a fox running for cover."

Clarinda laughed, she could not help it. She always enjoyed the Dowager's dry humour.

"She looked very beautiful," she remarked.

"That is a matter of opinion," the Dowager replied sharply. "Go and lie down, child. I want you to look your best tonight for your first visit to Carlton House."

Obediently Clarinda went to her room, but she did not immediately ring for Betty. She sat looking at herself in the long mirror, noting the way that her red-gold hair framed her face beneath her high bonnet and seeing the whiteness of her skin against the blue of her gown.

It seemed impossible, she thought, that this could be Clarinda Vernon, the girl who had been ashamed of her shabby gowns, who had gone for years without having a new dress and who had had to patch and darn every garment she possessed.

Now her wardrobe was full of new clothes of every sort and description, all extremely expensive and all in the height of fashion.

Although she rejoiced in owning them, Clarinda could not help remembering the agony she had suffered during her first week in London. She had to stand for hour after hour while materials were pinned around her.

She travelled from shop to shop while the Dowager bought, despite her protests and a guilty feeling that she should not be spending so much money on herself, what seemed to be an avalanche of bonnets, reticules, pelisses, slippers, gloves and wraps.

However the result, she had to admit, was sensational. She had been acclaimed a beauty from the first moment she had appeared amongst the *Beau Ton*.

Although she tried to be cynical and tell herself it was only because she was labelled an heiress that everyone was so pleasant to her, she had to admit that the whole glittering facade of Society was fascinating and unbelievably entertaining.

She certainly had no time for any introspection. When she was not purchasing clothes or having dancing lessons, she and the Dowager Marchioness were being entertained at almost every hour of the day.

There were not only balls, but Receptions, assemblies, smaller gatherings where people conversed and listened to music, luncheon parties and dinner parties, besides the time taken up with innumerable callers paying respects to the Dowager while keeping an eye admiringly on Clarinda.

"When gentlemen compliment me," she said to the Dowager soon after she arrived in London, "I cannot help feeling that they are roasting me. I am not used to flattery."

"You must learn to accept a compliment gracefully," the Dowager admonished her.

"I try," Clarinda admitted, "although sometimes I want to laugh. When young men go into eulogies about my eyebrows or the shape of my nose, I cannot help feeling how idiotic they sound."

"You will get used to it," the Dowager said wisely.

And after nearly a month in London Clarinda had to admit that she was right!

She was beginning to find it quite easy to accept all the complimentary phrases that were whispered in her ear at every party and she became used to seeing a look of excitement in a man's eyes as he raised her hand to his lips.

She grew quite adept at avoiding an offer of marriage except from those who were too persistent or thick-skinned to take a hint.

However what never ceased to surprise her was that she saw so little of Lord Melburne. She could hardly believe it possible that she could live in a man's house, know that he was her host and, more important still, her Guardian, and yet have little or no direct contact with him.

When they did meet, it was always in the presence of others, either his grandmother was present or it was a dinner party. Even when he accompanied them to dinner at other people's houses, it seemed to Clarinda almost extraordinary that they were never seated next to each other and he never asked her to dance.

She had been very angry with Lord Melburne when they first came to London and she had thought that she would find herself continually raging at him, incensed by his proprietary attitude and fighting with him in words like the cut-and-thrust of a duel with swords.

On the contrary the situation was almost deflating and in a way frustrating, but she had no chance of even arguing with him about anything.

He was always courteous in a detached indifferent manner and she was well aware that she should be grateful to him for the comforts she enjoyed at Melburne

House. But she felt now that it must be intentional on his part that they should never be alone together.

She received occasional messages from him through his grandmother. It was in this way that she learnt that should anyone unsuitable make her an offer of marriage, she had only to tell the gentleman in question to call on her Guardian and Lord Melburne would blight any hopes he might have had of gaining her hand.

Clarinda discovered that the only way to communicate such matters to Lord Melburne was to send him a note, and duly in the morning before she and the Dowager started their round of gaiety for the day she would write in her elegant hand a few words on a sheet of writing paper.

"Lord Wilmot will be calling on you today, my Lord, I have no wish to accept his suit."

Or,

"Captain Charles Cuddington may well ask your Lordship's permission to see me alone, please prevent this if possible."

Lord Melburne never replied, but Clarinda found that the young men she disliked were barred the house and even made no effort to approach her again when they saw her at other parties.

She felt that Lord Melburne was extremely thorough in the execution of his duties as her Guardian, but that he appeared to have no desire to communicate personally with her.

Before she came to London that was exactly what she would have desired and yet now his attitude of indifference piqued her although she would not admit this to herself.

When she was dressed ready for dinner at Carlton House, Betty exclaimed her delight at her appearance,

"You look lovely, Miss Clarinda," she said, "even lovelier than you looked last night. I wish you could have heard all those nice things that were said about you, miss,"

Clarinda glanced at her reflection in the mirror. Her dress for tonight's party was green, a soft green of buds in early spring, and for a moment she thought that her gown, with its tiny brilliants like drops of water, made her look like a nymph rising from the lake at Melburne.

Then she remembered that she had been wearing a green gown the night Nicholas had taken her to the caves. She gave a little shudder.

Could green be unlucky she wondered? And told herself that she was being nonsensical.

"I am very proud of you, child," the Dowager smiled as they walked downstairs.

Lord Melburne was waiting for them in the hall, looking incredibly handsome with the decorations that he had won in the Army glittering on the blue satin of his evening coat.

Clarinda looked up at him hoping to see some glint of admiration in his eyes. She had become experienced enough now to recognise that particular expression which sometimes held a flicker of fire behind it.

But Lord Melburne seemed preoccupied in brushing a speck of dust from his sleeve and it was at his grandmother he looked rather than at his Ward.

"We must not be late," he said, "you know how the Prince insists that his dinner parties shall start on time, especially when it is to be followed by a large Reception."

"We have plenty of time," the Dowager suggested soothingly. "I am looking forward to hearing what Clarinda thinks of Carlton House."

"Of course, it is her first visit," Lord Melburne said. "I had forgotten that. I hope she will not expect too much or she may well be disappointed."

"But everything is so exciting for me!" Clarinda exclaimed, wondering why he spoke of her as if she was not present.

"You will find Prinny's parties unbearably hot and invariably a tiresome crush," Lord Melburne said in a bored voice. "If I could avoid such occasions, I certainly would."

"I hope you are not coming tonight solely on my account," Clarinda said shyly.

"No, indeed," Lord Melburne replied. "The Prince of Wales insisted on my presence. He likes to have his most intimate friends around him when he entertains."

Lord Melburne's reply was quite crushing and Clarinda lapsed into silence.

Carlton House was, however, even more impressive than she had expected. From the moment she entered the Corinthian portico, she felt that she gaped like a yokel at the pillars of porphyry in the hall, at Chinese yellow silk hangings in the drawing room and at the busts, statues, griffins and urns.

She felt so stunned by the dining room walls of silver supported by columns in red and yellow granite that it was hard at first for her to eat or converse with the gentlemen on either side of her.

The dinner was long and elaborate with innumerable French dishes served on solid silver plates, but, when it was over, there were more marvels to see outside.

Through the Rose Satin Room festooned with flowers and the adjoining anteroom with its frieze of sphinxes encircling the bust of Minerva, there was a vast conservatory with a buffet creaking under a load of gold ornaments.

Supper tables were laid out in the garden, where there were miniature fountains and a cascade in which flashed gold and silver fish and there were fairy lamps and Chinese lanterns to illuminate the velvet-smooth lawns.

For Clarinda there was also the novelty of staring at the guests, who were even more colourful than their host's collection of famous pictures. The women in high-waisted gowns of satin, gauze or muslin, damped to show every curve of their sinuous figures were, with their magnificent tiaras and glittering necklaces, no less colourful than the men in their white knee-breeches and their satin coats embellished with bejewelled decorations.

Never in her wildest dreams had Clarinda imagined anything could be so beautiful, so gay and so noisy. And what was more exciting was that she could never stand for a moment by the Dowager's side before someone asked her to dance.

It was very hot and the thousands of candles made it hotter still. Lord Melburne slipped away from the elite circle round the Prince of Wales to find a quiet place by a window where he could sit down with three friends to a game of cards.

He was therefore somewhat surprised to find a small figure standing beside him and to hear a low voice say,

"Could you please take me – home, my Lord?"

He glanced up in surprise and then rose to his feet.

"Take you home, Clarinda! It is not yet one o'clock. No one leaves a party at Carlton House until it is dawn!"

"I would like to retire, if it please you," Clarinda insisted, "But I cannot for the moment find your grandmother."

Lord Melburne glanced down at Clarinda's face enquiringly and then put his cards down on the table.

"I regret, gentlemen," he said to those he was playing with, "but my Ward has need of me."

"I wish she had need of me!" one of the gentlemen remarked, but Clarinda had already turned away from the table.

Lord Melburne followed her.

"What is the matter?" he asked when they were out of hearing.

"I cannot tell you – here," she replied, "but please say – nothing to your grandmother. I must leave – *I must.*"

Efficiently Lord Melburne found the Dowager sitting with some of her old cronies in one of the salons, drew her aside and told her that Clarinda wished to go home.

In what seemed to be an incredibly short time they were driving back towards Berkeley Square.

"You must be unwell to wish to leave so early," the Dowager said to Clarinda, "but I am delighted to get away from the heat and deafening clatter of the bands,"

"I have a slight headache," Clarinda admitted.

"It is not surprising," the Dowager replied, "you were late last night. Two big parties one on top of each other is too much for anyone,"

When they reached Melburne House, the Dowager gave a sigh.

"I must admit I welcome a chance to get to bed early," she said. "Come along, Clarinda. Send Betty for a glass of milk to help you to get to sleep."

"Perhaps I could just have a glass of lemonade," Clarinda said and looked appealingly at Lord Melburne.

"Come and have it in the library," he suggested. "I will not keep her long, Grandmama, I promise you."

"The sooner the child gets to bed the better," the Dowager replied.

She continued to move up the stairway and Clarinda walked with Lord Melburne to the library.

The big book-lined room seemed cold after all the excessive heat of Carlton House and Lord Melburne told one of the footmen to light the fire. He then went to the grog tray to pour Clarinda out a glass of lemonade.

She took it from him and set it down on a small table by the sofa. The footman left the room and she said in a hesitating voice,

"I have done – something very wrong – you will be very angry with me – and so will your grandmother,"

"Will you not sit down?" Lord Melburne asked.

Clarinda ignored the sofa that he indicated and sank down on the hearthrug. He settled himself in a winged armchair, looking exceedingly elegant as he sat watching her.

The flickering flames of the newly lit fire glinted on her hair, making it seem as if there were little tongues of fire flickering over her bent head. Her shimmering green dress billowed out around her and her bare shoulders were very white in the light of the candles.

"What have you done?" Lord Melburne wanted to know and his voice was kind.

"I have – insulted the – Duke of Kingston," Clarinda replied. "It was – wrong of me and I should not have behaved in such a – reprehensible way – but I warned you that you would – never make a – fashionable lady out of me."

"How did you insult him?" Lord Melburne asked.

"I hardly like to – tell you," Clarinda said, "for your grandmother only today told me how important he is. She is very impressed by – His Grace and she was so delighted that last night he asked me to dance. Now I have – offended him and he may tell the Prince how – badly I have behaved. I am sure I shall never be – asked to – Carlton House again."

"Would that worry you very much?" Lord Melburne enquired.

"I suppose not," Clarinda answered. "But it would upset your grandmother – who has been so – kind to me and it might be – uncomfortable for you."

"What have you done?" Lord Melburne asked her again.

Then, before Clarinda could reply, he said,

"Start at the beginning. Did the Duke ask you to dance?"

Clarinda nodded.

"Yes," she replied. "I danced with several other gentlemen and I saw that His Grace was standing at the side of the ballroom watching me. Then he came up to me and insisted that it was his dance, although I had promised it to someone else."

"I am sure that His Grace was very persuasive," Lord Melburne remarked in a sarcastic voice.

"He was not persuasive, just overbearing," Clarinda then corrected him. "He seemed to assume it was his right to dance with me."

"So you danced with him," Lord Melburne prompted.

"I did not have very much choice in the matter," Clarinda replied. "He took me almost forcibly onto the floor. It was very hot and overcrowded and, when he stopped dancing, I was glad."

"So you walked in the garden," Lord Melburne said as if he knew the inevitable end of the story.

Clarinda nodded again as she was gazing into the flames with her head bowed.

There was a silence and after a moment Lord Melburne said,

"What happened?"

Because she was embarrassed, Clarinda stammered as she answered,

"He tried to k-kiss me – and when I protested he did not seem to h-hear me, so I ran – away."

She paused for a moment before she went on,

"He ran after me – I don't know why – it was s-stupid of me, but I was f-frightened. He was so big, I thought he was going to catch me – and then I ran into one of the buffets. You know how they stretched out into the garden. There did not seem to be many people there – and I thought he might s-seize hold of me and drag me – away, so I – "

Her voice died away.

"What did you do?" Lord Melburne asked.

"I picked up a — bowl of fruit salad," Clarinda admitted miserably, "and threw it — over him."

There was a moment's silence before Lord Melburne put back his head and laughed aloud.

"Always the unexpected where you are concerned, Clarinda!" he exclaimed. "If only I could have seen His Grace's face!"

Clarinda looked at him for the first time.

"You are not — angry?" she asked.

"Not in the slightest," Lord Melburne replied. "He deserved it."

"But your — grandmother?"

"I very much doubt whether Grandmama or anyone else will know what happened unless you tell them. No man likes to look a fool and His Grace is very conscious of his dignity."

"Supposing he — tells the Prince?" Clarinda asked.

"He will not. I am absolutely convinced, Clarinda, that he will say nothing about this to anyone. He would look too foolish. No man is at his best covered in fruit salad!"

Clarinda gave a deep sigh.

"I hope you are — right. I have been feeling so — ashamed of myself. It is my terrible temper. You know how I say and do anything — when I am angry."

"I do indeed," Lord Melburne remarked meaningfully and she blushed.

For a few moments he sat watching her before he asked,

"Did you have any more adventures tonight?"

"Lord Carloss offered for me," she replied in a low voice. "I told him to come and see you tomorrow."

"Johnny Carloss!" Lord Melburne exclaimed. "He is a very decent chap, a sportsman and exceeding warm in the pocket. He is most certainly not concerned with your money. Are you interested in him?"

"No," Clarinda replied.

"Why not?" Lord Melburne enquired.

"He is too immature," she answered.

"I beg your pardon!" Lord Melburne exclaimed in surprise.

"I said," Clarinda repeated, "he is too immature."

"Do you know the meaning of the word?" Lord Melburne then asked. "John Carloss is twenty-seven if he is a day. You are – I think – just nineteen!"

"I am sorry if it seems to you that I am being presumptuous, but his Grace admitted to me that he never reads a book from one year's end to another. You might well think of him as a sportsman, but, although I am sure that he tools his horses well, he would have no idea of what to do if one strained a fetlock. He has never studied the breeding of his racehorses, he only knows if they win or lose. And, although he goes frequently to Newmarket, he had no idea until I told him that the Racecourse was started in the reign of King Charles II."

"Do you think a knowledge of those things is important in a husband?" Lord Melburne asked, his eyes twinkling.

"Surely if one is married one sometimes has intelligent conversations?" Clarinda replied.

"Grandmama was afraid that you were a female with a brainbox," Lord Melburne said. "I am beginning to think she was right."

"I cannot help the way I was brought up," Clarinda parried hotly.

"Would it be impertinent to ask how you were educated?" Lord Melburne enquired.

"My father or rather Lawrence Vernon, whose name I bear, was a scholar."

"I had no idea," Lord Melburne remarked.

"He thought only of his books, which was why we were so poor," Clarinda explained. "He was determined that I should be well read. I had studied most of the Classics by the time I was twelve, I could repeat all the great speeches in Shakespeare's plays by heart and by the time I was fifteen, when Papa was killed, I was quite proficient in Latin and Greek."

"A boy's education in fact."

"Exactly," Clarinda agreed. "And as he had no son, Papa taught me to ride and shoot,"

"To shoot!" Lord Melburne exclaimed.

She glanced up at him with laughter in her eyes.

"I have often thought that I would like to challenge your Lordship in the snipe bog at The Priory," she said.

"I accept your challenge," he replied promptly, "and we will have a return match where the wild ducks fly in the North-West corner of Melburne."

"I often went partridge shooting with Sir Roderick and last time we were out I got fifteen brace to his – "

She stopped.

"I have no wish to boast, my Lord, it might shorten the odds against me."

Lord Melburne laughed.

Then he said,

"In shooting at least you would find a companionship with quite a number of the men who have offered for you. But you were telling me about your education and what happened after you were fifteen?"

"Uncle Roderick was interested in very different things from Papa," Clarinda said. "I think I know every detail of every campaign that Marlborough fought and because he was so interested in wars I read to him nearly all the books we could find in French on that subject. We covered the history of France as well and, of course, everything we could possibly glean about Napoleon himself."

She gave an exasperated sigh.

"I suppose you will think it regrettable that I can speak German and can follow Italian Operas without translation?"

"Grandmama would be horrified!"

"It is not fair," Clarinda complained. "She is proud enough of you."

"What do you mean?" he asked.

"She does not mind your having a brain," Clarinda said resentfully.

"How do you know I have one?" he enquired.

"You achieved a degree at Oxford University and, when I sat next to General Sir David Dundas at dinner the other night, he told me that, if you had not left the Army, he was quite convinced that with your genius for tactics you had every chance of eventually becoming the Commander-in-Chief."

"Sir David was flattering me," Lord Melburne demurred.

"Have you not thought," Clarinda said suddenly, "that the reason you become so bored with all the lovely ladies that gossip links you with is that they are incredibly empty-headed?"

"Who said I was bored?" Lord Melburne asked sharply.

Clarinda laughed.

"Do you imagine that it is not common knowledge?" she enquired. "Why, they have bets below the stairs as to how long your latest 'bit of muslin' will last! The knife boy won the last pool because no one else imagined it would be over within a month."

"Clarinda," Lord Melburne thundered. "How dare you repeat the servants' tattle-tattle! And you should not even know the expression, 'bit of muslin', let alone speak of it."

"But it is true that you are bored. And it is not only because I have listened to servants' gossip that I know about it. When we were at the Opera the other night – you know how there is only a curtain dividing some of the boxes – I heard two gentlemen talking. One of them said, 'that is the little love bird who interests me, the third from the right, the dark one with green eyes.'

"'The other man replied, 'you will have to hurry, Harry, I saw Buck Melburne talking to her last night.' 'Damme,' the first man exclaimed. 'He always pips me at the post. He took Liane away from me. I swore I would get even with him for that'."

There was a pause in the conversation before Harry added,

"'He is never interested for long. And I find that quite useful not being as deep in the pocket as you are Buck.

The 'ladybirds' are so distressed when Buck gets bored with them at being propelled back into circulation so quickly, that poor men like myself can pick them up at bargain prices!'"

"*Clarinda!*" Lord Melburne said in an even angrier tone. "Did your extensive education ever include a good spanking?"

"Papa always said," Clarinda replied demurely, "that a man who had to use brute force instead of reason is a nitwit."

"Nitwit or not," Lord Melburne said grimly, "if you drive me too far, you will be sorry!"

She glanced up at him, saw the squareness of his chin and anger smouldering in his eyes and capitulated.

"I have had a shaking from you, my Lord," she said in a low voice. "I have no wish for another."

Then suddenly the blood rose in her cheeks as she remembered what had happened after he had shaken her.

"Then don't listen to such conversations," Lord Melburne insisted reprovingly and in the tone of a man who is tried almost beyond endurance.

"How can I help it?" Clarinda asked. "What you really mean is that I should not repeat them to you."

"No. I don't mean that!" Lord Melburne contradicted her fiercely. "I want you to be very frank with me. What I would really dislike is if you were to lie to me. Somehow, Clarinda, I feel you would not do that."

"Of course I would not," she retorted. "Why should I?"

"No reason at all. I trust you to tell me the truth," he replied. "But, then damn it all, you should not hear talk

~177~

of 'ladybirds' and such like. You are an innocent *debutante*!"

"A reluctant one, as you well know. But don't talk about me, we were talking about you and why you get bored so easily."

"I will not discuss anything you have learnt by eavesdropping," he said crushingly.

"But you are often bored, are you not, my Lord?" Clarinda insisted, "But then I am not surprised. You were right about one thing, I find the Social world far more fascinating and amusing than I had expected. But I am convinced that a great number of the people in it are excessively stupid."

"You sound just as if you are as old and wise as Methuselah," Lord Melburne said and almost despite himself there was an amused twinkle in his eyes.

"Sometimes I feel that I am," Clarinda replied. "I was watching a young man gaming the other night. He had won a small fortune and the mathematical chances against his continuing to win must have been astronomical. Yet he stayed at the table, playing and playing until he had lost the lot. Do you not think that was ridiculously foolish?"

"I am becoming worried about you, Clarinda," Lord Melburne said. "If you continue to be so critical, how shall Grandmama and I ever find a husband to please you?"

There was a pause before Clarinda asked in a very small voice,

"You would not – make me marry anyone I did not like?"

"Of course not! I would never force any man upon you."

"Then I will be brave and tell you that however important socially a gentleman might be, I would never marry unless I was in love."

"Do you know what love is?" Lord Melburne asked.

"No," she answered. "Do you?"

She then looked up at him with a hint of mischief in her eyes, as if once again she was deliberately trying to provoke him. But there was an expression in his grey eyes that made her suddenly become very still.

They looked at each other, the firelight flickering on their faces and it just seemed to Clarinda that something that she had never known before passed between them. Something that awoke a strange feeling deep within her heart.

It was exciting and thrilling and it made it hard for her to breathe.

"Clarinda," he asked very softly, "do you not think that we could be friends?"

For a moment or two she carried on looking at him with her dark blue eyes very wide in her little heart-shaped face, the firelight glimmering on her hair and her lips parted.

Then, it seemed to be with an effort, she looked away from him.

"No! *No!*" she cried out. "There is – something that stops – me, that will always – stop me and you know what it is."

"Jessica Tansley," Lord Melburne said almost beneath his breath.

"Yes – Jessica," Clarinda whispered.

Then, before he could move, she had risen and ran as swiftly as a frightened fawn from the room.

CHAPTER NINE

"I thought we were to drive in Hyde Park this afternoon," Clarinda said to the Dowager, as they set off in an open carriage from Berkeley Square.

"That is what I had intended," the Dowager replied, "but I had a note this morning from the Duchess of Devonshire asking us to tea this afternoon. Her Grace was so pressing that I thought it would be discourteous not to accept her hospitality."

"I am delighted you did," Clarinda answered, "I am much looking forward to seeing Devonshire House."

"You will find it a page out of history. The Devonshires have played their part in this country's affairs for so many generations that Devonshire House has become the focal point of every important political and national event."

"I noticed the Duchess at Carlton House," Clarinda said. "She is very beautiful."

"And a compulsive gambler," the Dowager added in a dry voice.

"I often wonder what makes people gamble so feverishly," Clarinda remarked almost to herself and then added, "I know the answer – it is because they are bored."

She thought of Lord Melburne and remembered their conversation of last night. He had been unexpectedly very kind, she thought. She had expected him to be incensed with her, but instead he had been understanding and even amused.

At the same time Clarinda could not help hoping that the Dowager would not hear of the escapade. She would certainly not think it funny that the Duke of Kingston had been treated in such a cavalier fashion.

Besides, Clarinda thought nervously, if the Dowager heard that His Grace had tried to kiss her, she would feel it was another step forward in her ambitions that he should declare his suit.

"Who do you think might be at tea with the Duchess?" Clarinda asked, anxious not to pursue the trend of her own thoughts.

"I have no idea," the Dowager replied. "Were you hoping to meet anyone in particular?"

She looked at Clarinda with shrewd eyes as she asked the question and Clarinda bit back an impulse to say that there was no one she particularly wanted to meet, but there was one person who she had no wish to see again and that was the Duke of Kingston.

It was a short distance from Melburne House to the Devonshires' magnificent residence in Piccadilly. The horses turned in at the great wrought-iron gold-tipped gates and drew up at the porticoed front door.

"It appears to be quite a small party," the Dowager remarked, looking around for other carriages as she stepped out of her own.

Clarinda did not answer. She was already awestruck as they entered the hall by the huge curving staircase which divided into two wings at a landing where stood a gigantic marble statue.

There were endless over-sized portraits of the Devonshires, each member of the family appearing, according to their sex, more handsome or more beautiful than the last and, when Clarinda and the Dowager had ascended the staircase, they entered the exquisitely furnished salon overlooking the garden where the Duchess was receiving her friends.

With her red-gold hair, her pink and white complexion and chiselled features, Georgina, Duchess of Devonshire, was even lovelier than the many portraits that had immortalised her for posterity.

Holding out her hand to the Dowager she moved forward with indescribable grace and kissed the older woman on both cheeks.

"I am so delighted that you could come, ma'am," she said effusively. "And I have been so looking forward to meeting the most talked of *debutante* of the Season, your grandson's Ward."

She held out her hand to Clarinda, who sank down in a deep curtsey.

"Come and tell me how much you enjoy being such a success," she said beguilingly and Clarinda thought that she had never seen more expressive eyes in any woman.

There was a number of distinguished people present and the Duchess presented Clarinda. Then, turning to a tall good-looking young man, whom she had introduced as 'my husband's nephew', she suggested,

"George, do take Miss Vernon and show her the garden. I am convinced that she would be more interested in seeing the flowers, which are really lovely this year, than in listening to the scandalous gossip that we old cronies are determined to indulge in."

Clarinda could not help smiling at the Duchess describing herself as 'old'. She looked so vividly alive, so youthful with her flashing smile and quick movements that it was impossible to think of her as anything but a young girl.

But Clarinda was far too shy to express such sentiments and obediently she followed the young gentleman whose features were clearly those of a Cavendish, down the staircase and out into the garden.

"Are you enjoying yourself in London?" he asked conventionally.

"Very much indeed," Clarinda replied, "but I would not like to live in a City all the year round. I miss the freedom of the country and the chance of galloping a horse without feeling, as one does in Hyde Park, a fear of offending the conventions and, of course, the peace of a garden and meadows and fields."

"In which case, you are very unusual," he said. "Most females have an insatiable desire for the balls, the parties and the excitement of London, but personally I agree with you, a little is enough."

They both laughed as if he had said something rather funny.

Then, looking around at the flower beds all ablaze with blossom, the yew trees elegantly fashioned by topiary and the long green lawns smooth as plush and the great oak and lime trees, Clarinda exclaimed,

"One might be in the country here!"

As she spoke, she pulled her glove off her right hand to touch the velvety petal of a white rose.

"It is indeed an oasis in the turmoil of a City which is growing bigger year by year," Mr. Cavendish smiled. "I often feel that there will soon be no room for gardens unless one drives miles to find them."

"It would be so tragic," Clarinda said, "if the great mansions like Devonshire House of which I have seen so many since I have been in London – should disappear. They have a grandeur and elegance all of their own."

"I see you have a feeling for such things," Mr. Cavendish said earnestly. "Would you allow me, Miss Vernon, to – "

What he was about to say Clarinda never knew, for at that very moment she heard a step behind them. She turned round and then started wide-eyed and apprehensive.

It was the Duke of Kingston who stood there, looking, Clarinda thought nervously, larger and more overpowering than ever.

He was immaculately dressed, but his face was rather pink as if he had been hurrying.

When he had bowed to Clarinda, he put a hand on Mr. Cavendish's shoulder.

"Your aunt is asking for you, dear boy. She asked me to tell you that she requires your presence immediately in the salon."

"I thank you, Your Grace. I will go to her at once," Mr. Cavendish replied.

He bowed to Clarinda. She saw the expression in his eyes and knew that he was telling her wordlessly how disappointed he was that they could no longer continue to converse.

"Your servant, Miss Vernon," he said politely.

Then he was walking away across the green lawn, leaving her alone with the Duke.

'This has all been arranged,' she thought and looked up at him nervously.

"I think – I owe Your Grace – an apology – " she began, but before she could say more he reached out and took her ungloved hand in his.

"You have spirit," he boomed in his rather loud voice, "and I like women with spirit. I should be angry with you for serving me such a scully trick at Carlton House last night! But you captivated me from the moment I first saw you and now it would be impossible for me to do anything but love you,"

"Please – Your Grace," Clarinda pleaded shyly, trying to take her hand away from him.

"You are entrancing," he said. "I cannot kiss you here because it is too public, but I will talk to the Dowager and arrange that she brings you to dinner at my house tonight."

"It is not – possible. I am – sure we have another – engagement!" Clarinda cried, feeling that somehow he was overpowering her and sapping her resistance in an inexplicable manner and making her feel weak and defenceless.

"We have a lot of plans to make – you and I, Clarinda," the Duke smiled. "I have already spoken to the Prince of Wales and he says that the second of July will suit him well, before he goes to Brighthelmstone. Can you be ready by then? I promise you I shall be a very impatient bridegroom."

"I don't – know what you are – saying," Clarinda protested desperately.

"I am talking about our Wedding," he replied. "It will be a very grand affair, Clarinda. And the Queen will be present, also the King if His Majesty's health permits and naturally the Prince will be my Best Man,"

"Our – Wedding!" Clarinda exclaimed breathlessly. "I am – afraid, Your Grace – you must d-discuss this with – my Guardian – Lord Melburne,"

"You are being very conventional, my dear," he replied, "and I like you for it. It is what I would wish my wife to be. But I can assure you that I can be conventional too. I have already spoken to Lord Melburne and he has given his permission to our marriage."

"He has – given his – permission!" Clarinda found that she could hardly enunciate the words.

"But of course! Now there are no obstacles in our path, so let's make plans accordingly for, as I have already told you, I am impatient, very impatient, to hold you in my arms."

"I c-cannot – I cannot – believe – " Clarinda, began, stammering in her agitation.

"That I love you," he interrupted her. "My dearest, it is the truth. I fell in love with you at first sight."

"But – I cannot – " Clarinda tried to say.

"And now that you have promised to marry me," the Duke continued, "I am returning immediately to Berkeley Square to tell your Guardian that the Ceremony will take place on the second of July and that you must be ready by then, for even if His Royal Highness had not approved the date, I could have waited no longer."

He raised Clarinda's hand, which he had held in his while he spoke, to his lips and she felt his mouth hot, possessive and somehow greedy on the softness of her skin.

With a little cry like that of a captured animal, Clarinda wrenched herself free of him and turning ran away across the garden.

He watched her go with a smile on his lips.

"So young, so unspoilt," he said aloud. "It will be a pleasure to conquer her," and as if Clarinda's shyness had excited him, he walked slowly back to the house looking very pleased with himself.

Clarinda reached the front door and realised that Lord Melburne's carriage was not there. She knew that the coachman, expecting them to stay very much longer, would be walking the horses and, refusing a footman's suggestion that he should call her a Hackney cab, she said quickly,

"I will walk."

Ignoring the expression of astonishment on the servant's face, she moved quickly across the courtyard and into Piccadilly.

As soon as she had turned a few moments later into Berkeley Street, she started to run. Picking up the front of her gown, regardless of curious looks from the passers-by, she sped as quickly as she could down the long Street into Berkeley Square.

It only took her five minutes to reach Melburne House and the door was opened by a footman even as she put her hand up towards the knocker.

She swept past him, saw the Major Domo, who was standing in the hall looking at her in surprise, and asked with difficulty,

"His – Lordship – is he – here?"

"I believe his Lordship is in the library, miss," the Major Domo replied and Clarinda, without waiting for a footman to precede her, ran down the hall and flung open the library door.

She slammed it to behind her and stood leaning against the polished mahogany, panting from the speed that she had been running at.

Her bonnet had fallen back and was caught only by the ribbons round her throat. Her hair had become dishevelled in the wind and rioted in soft curls around her forehead. Her cheeks were flushed. The laces at her breast rose and fell tumultuously.

Lord Melburne had been sitting at his desk writing a letter. He stared at Clarinda with raised eyebrows and then rose slowly to his feet.

But before he could speak, Clarinda cried, her breath coming in broken gasps,

"*You – lied to me*! You have – broken your promise. I did not – believe – you could be so despicable – so two-faced – after what you said last night. But you – lied to me and now he is coming here – he is on his way – I swear to you I will – not do it whatever you may – say to me – I will not, I will not marry him!"

She paused for lack of breath and Lord Melburne, staring at her in amazement, then said slowly in his most uncompromising voice,

"May I enquire the reason for this incomprehensible flapdoodle?"

"He is – coming to – you now," Clarinda reiterated. "He has it – all arranged – for the second of July – but I will not marry – him! Do you hear me? I will not – marry him! If you – dragged me up – the aisle I swear – I will still say 'no' when I reach – the Altar steps."

"Would you kindly enlighten me as to who is on his way here?" Lord Melburne asked.

"As if – you did not know – the answer!" Clarinda said scornfully. "It is the – Duke of Kingston and. His Grace should be – here at any second!"

Lord Melburne crossed the room with unhurried dignity to pull the bell. Almost at once the door was opened behind Clarinda and the Major Domo stood there.

"If anyone should call," Lord Melburne ordered, "I am not at home and you are not expecting me to return until after six of the clock."

"Very good, my Lord."

The door was closed again.

"You look extremely dishevelled, Clarinda," Lord Melburne said coldly. "Perhaps you would wish to tidy yourself before we continue our conversation."

Clarinda reached up her hands, tugged at the ribbons of her bonnet and then flung the expensive headgear onto the floor.

"No!" she answered angrily. "My appearance is – not of the least – consequence. I wish to know – why should you should break – your promise to me within only a few hours of – making it. Why you should try to – marry me to a man whom I do not even – like and who – frightens me."

She was now not quite so breathless, but her words still came jerkily from between her lips and Lord Melburne, going to the grog tray, poured out a glass of lemonade.

"Suppose you sit down," he said quietly, "and let us discuss this in a civilised manner."

"I will not – marry him – *I will – not*," Clarinda asserted strongly through gritted teeth.

She took the glass of lemonade from Lord Melburne's hands and sipped it thirstily.

"Would it be indiscreet," he asked with a slight twinkle in his eye, "to ask why you are so out of breath? Can it be that you have run all the way here from Devonshire House?"

"I had – to arrive – before His – Grace," Clarinda explained.

"I always thought that the Duke overestimated the performance of his horseflesh," Lord Melburne remarked drily and he was smiling.

"Don't laugh at me!" Clarinda cried furiously. "You deceived me by – promising that you would never – force any – man on me – and now you have given your permission for my – marriage with the Duke."

"I have done nothing of the sort," Lord Melburne replied.

Clarinda looked up at him, her eyes suspicious.

"But His Grace – told me that you – had. He has just – said so!"

"I only gave His Grace permission to ask for your hand in marriage," Lord Melburne corrected her. "That I could not refuse, Clarinda. He is, as you know, completely eligible and it is not in my power to forbid anyone without any reason to approach you as a prospective bridegroom. But you have complete freedom to accept or refuse any offer you receive."

"But he – told me – "

The Duke is, not surprisingly, a very conceited man," Lord Melburne said quietly. "It would never enter his head that any woman, especially one as comparatively unimportant as yourself, Clarinda, would refuse him."

"Then I don't – have to marry – him?" Clarinda asked in a very small voice.

"Not as far as I am concerned," Lord Melburne replied.

"Then will – you tell him – so?" Clarinda asked, "for I know His Grace will not – listen to me."

"If you empower me to refuse the Duke's suit, then I shall do so," Lord Melburne said, "although I feel sure that, even from my lips, he will find it very hard to credit."

Clarinda put down the glass of lemonade she held on a table beside her and put her hands up to her hair.

"I know I should not have – run away from – Devonshire House," she said humbly. "Your grandmother will be – incensed with me, but I was so – afraid."

" – and so angry with me," Lord Melburne added.

"I thought you had – betrayed me."

"Did you really think I would make you marry that blustering windbag!" Lord Melburne exclaimed.

She stared at him wide-eyed.

"I had thought that – just like your grandmother you – wanted me to make an – important marriage."

"I want you to be happy," Lord Melburne replied, "but I should not be doing my duty as your Guardian, Clarinda, if I did not point out to you the advantages of such a union."

It seemed to Clarinda that he already regretted the belittling way he had spontaneously spoken about the Duke.

Now he walked across the room and back again before he said,

"Do you really understand what you are refusing besides the man himself? You would have a unique position in Society, Clarinda. You would have the nearest place to Royalty that a commoner can hold. You would be immensely rich, envied, fêted, admired wherever you might go. There is not, I believe, any girl in the whole length and breadth of this country who would not jump at the chance to marry His Grace of Kingston."

"But I don't – love him," Clarinda said in a low voice.

"And you think that matters more than anything else?" Lord Melburne asked.

She saw he was looking at her searchingly with those penetrating grey eyes, which made her feel always that he looked deep into the heart of a person, seeking for something that was not apparent on the surface and looking, as it were, into their very heart and soul.

"I could not – let him – touch me," she whispered and shivered.

"Then on your behalf I will refuse His Grace's kind offer," Lord Melburne said firmly. "Don't perturb yourself, Clarinda. I promise you he will not worry you again."

"But your – grandmother," Clarinda faltered.

"I will deal with Grandmama as well," Lord Melburne said. "She also wants you to be happy, Clarinda. Unfortunately, like most of her generation, she is much more concerned that a marriage should be advantageous from a worldly point of view than that one should know the joys of loving and being loved."

Clarinda drew a deep breath as if her relief at what Lord Melburne was now saying was inexpressible.

Then she looked up at him with a little smile and murmured,

"I am – sorry."

"For what?" he enquired.

"For being rude," she answered. "It seems I must always be apologising to you, my Lord, whenever we are alone together."

"You perhaps had some provocation today."

"That is generous of you," she answered.

There was a silence and, because she knew he was gazing at her, she felt shy.

Nervously she put up her hands to smooth her curls and to tidy the laces at her breast.

She was suddenly conscious of the silence that lay between them, a silence which was somehow pregnant with a meaning which she could not understand and because she was so embarrassed she rushed hastily into speech without looking at him.

"I was thinking of you last night, my Lord."

"Of me?" Lord Melburne enquired.

"I was thinking of the things – we talked about. Most of all of your – boredom."

"You are making it quite a personal problem,"

"I was thinking," Clarinda went on, "that, while I have to hide away the fact that I have a brain of some sort, you have no reason to be ashamed of yours and so there are many things you could do which would keep you both occupied and interested."

"At the moment I am finding you almost a full-time occupation," he grinned.

Clarinda frowned.

"I am speaking seriously, my Lord."

"I beg your pardon if I sound frivolous," he replied, "but it happens to be a fact."

"I am thinking of your life in general," Clarinda said. "You know as well as I do that, if I engage some of your time now, it is only for a short period. Soon I shall have left London and returned to the country. Then what will you do?"

"What I have done before, I imagine," he answered. "Amuse myself."

"And yet you are not really amused," she said. "That is what causes me concern."

"I am deeply grateful for this most flattering attention on your part," Lord Melburne said with mock humility.

"Oh, don't be so irritating!" she flashed at him. "Can you not see I am just trying to help you? I have considered your problem and found, if you would like to hear them, at least one or two solutions."

Lord Melburne sat down in the chair opposite her with a twinkle at the back of his eyes. His voice was, however, quite serious as he said,

"I apologise again if I sounded frivolous. I am extremely curious as to what remedy you would prescribe for an occasional outburst of irrepressible boredom."

"Well, I was thinking firstly of all the things that you could do at Melburne."

"At Melburne?" his Lordship enquired with raised eyebrows. "Surely you are not saying that I should rebuild the house after my father has already done it so extravagantly? Or do you consider that Foster is not carrying out his duties satisfactorily?"

"I am sure that Major Foster is a very good Agent," Clarinda replied, "but he is merely carrying on the estate in the same well-conducted way that it was run in your father's time. So he would never attempt anything revolutionary without your permission or indeed, I am convinced, without your inspiration."

"And what innovations would you suggest I propose?" Lord Melburne asked.

It seemed to Clarinda that there was something almost hostile in his tone as if he resented her finding fault with his estate.

"These, of course, are only my own ideas," she said tremulously. "I am quite sure that your Lordship will have better ones."

"And what suggestions would you make?" Lord Melburne asked in the tone of voice of a man who thinks that the subject of discussion was not open to improvement.

"Well, first of all," Clarinda said, looking away from him, "the High Wood in the North-West corner has passed its prime – it needs replanting. It covers over two hundred acres, but it would be quite easy for you to build a timber yard on the spot and make a short road down to the highway. The granite pits are not far away and that part of your estate is badly in need of new cottages."

There was a moment's silence before Lord Melburne asked,

"And what else?"

"Everyone of import I have spoken to since I came to London," Clarinda went on, "like General Sir David Dundas, seems convinced that the Armistice is but an excuse for Napoleon to rearm. If the War is renewed, this country will once again be badly in need of food. If you cleared away the scrub from the land to the East of

Coombes Bottom and drained the Marsh, you could put nearly two thousand more acres into cultivation."

"How the devil do you know all this?" he asked. "I apologise for my language, Clarinda, but you surprise me."

"I have always been interested in the Melburne Estate," Clarinda answered, "and I could not help comparing the improvements that we were making every year with the unchanging conditions at Melburne. Uncle Roderick and I often thought that your management was just a trifle old-fashioned."

"Well, you have most certainly given me something to think about," he replied sharply. "Anything else?"

"You may not – like this – idea," Clarinda faltered, "but I heard last year and the year before that all the races you won were either at Epsom or at Ascot. Have you ever thought that instead of keeping your horses at Newmarket, which is far further from London than Melburne, it would be more convenient and far cheaper for you to train at home? Besides, now you have Dingle's Ride you have a perfect gallop ready-made.

She looked directly at Lord Melburne for the first time since she had been speaking and saw by the expression on his face that her last suggestion interested him.

"You have given me much to consider, Clarinda," he remarked after a moment.

"I have not quite – finished."

"More for me to do?" he enquired.

"A great deal more if you wish it," she answered. "You are a Member of the House of Lords. Have you never thought of how a Bill is urgently needed to prevent girls of thirteen and fourteen becoming prostitutes?"

Lord Melburne sat bolt upright.

"Who has been talking to you about such things?" he enquired.

"No one," Clarinda answered. "But I have the use of my eyes. I can see them standing in Piccadilly – miserable little creatures with painted faces, quite obviously attempting to attract the gentlemen who pass them."

"A lady of sensibility would not notice such things," Lord Melburne asserted positively.

"No, but a gentleman of sensibility should," she retorted. "Something should be done about them, just as I am convinced that a Law should be passed to prevent small climbing boys being forced to clean chimneys when they are often but five years old. I saw one the other day and he had large burns on his feet and legs and his face was streaked with tears. I was ashamed that such cruelty should be permitted in any civilised country."

Lord Melburne rose and walked across the room to the window.

"You are right, Clarinda," he said after a moment. "Of course you are right. But we have grown callous or else most of us are just thoughtless. Would it please you if I talked to their Lordships on such matters,"

"Perhaps nothing can be done," Clarinda answered, "but I cannot help feeling that men with brains like yourself, my Lord, should try to influence public opinion against some of the misery that one sees on every side in London. There is so much wealth, so much luxury and in contrast a poverty and a cruelty that has horrified me ever since I have been here."

"I thought you were enjoying yourself, Clarinda."

"I am, but although your grandmother would find it regrettable, I cannot help thinking at the same time."

"The brainbox in fact," Lord Melburne remarked.

"Exactly."

She glanced at the clock and Betty to her feet.

"Her Ladyship will be returning at any minute, my Lord, and I know that the Duke will have told her I ran away because he wished us to dine with him tonight. When she hears what you have to tell her, she may be angry with me and will most certainly be disappointed. Will you try to make her understand?"

"I promise you that I will do my best," Lord Melburne said. "Don't worry, Clarinda. I am certain that Grandmama, like myself, wants only one thing and that is your happiness."

There was a warmth in his voice that made Clarinda feel shy.

"Thank you, my Lord," she said softly, "and once again – please forgive me for being – rude."

She went from the room without waiting for his answers and, when she was upstairs, stayed for a moment with her hands to her face, feeling a relief like the warmth of sunshine steal over her. She knew now how afraid she had been of being forced to marry the Duke.

Then she rang the bell for Betty. She had already learnt from the Duchess that tonight would be the last of the great balls of the season. There would be a number of others, but the one given by the Earl and Countess of Hetherington at their mansion in Park Lane, would be, with the exception of Carlton House, the most glittering and the most important entertainment that Society could be invited to in London.

The Dowager had chosen a very special dress for Clarinda of white gauze. The frills that ornamented the hem were embroidered with turquoise beads. Turquoises also nestled in the lace that framed her shoulders and were even embroidered on her tiny white slippers.

"I have a present for you," the Dowager said when Clarinda went to her room rather apprehensively before going downstairs to dinner.

"A present for me, ma'am," Clarinda exclaimed.

She had expected to be greeted with reproaches. But at the Dowager's words she knew that Lord Melburne had smoothed her path and so she was not going to be taken to task for having refused the Duke.

"A present I hope you will like," the Dowager said and, opening a case on her dressing table, she held it out to Clarinda.

Against a black velvet background, Clarinda saw a necklace of turquoise and diamonds, a bracelet to match and small earrings fashioned in the shape of flowers.

"Oh, ma'am, is this really for me?" Clarinda cried.

"I intended to give it to you the night of your own ball," the Dowager said, "but then I thought it was far more suitable for the gown you are to wear tonight and so I kept it until now."

"Oh, thank you! *Thank you*! It is the loveliest thing I have ever seen and it is the first jewellery I have ever owned."

"I am glad you are pleased, child," the Dowager smiled.

"How can I ever thank you for all you have done for me?" Clarinda asked. "You have been so kind and I cannot tell you how happy it has made me to be with you. Sometimes it is almost like having Mama with me again."

"You could not say anything nicer. Thank you, child. Now put on your jewellery and so make yourself look even lovelier than you do already."

Clarinda certainly looked gay and happy as she went downstairs to greet the guests the Dowager had invited to dine with them. She knew most of them already and because she was in high spirits it seemed to her that there had never been a more amusing party since she first came to London.

When dinner was over, they all piled into the carriages waiting outside. Clarinda found herself travelling with the Dowager and noticed that she gave a little exclamation of pain as she sat down in the soft seat.

"Is your leg hurting you again, ma'am?" she enquired.

The Dowager nodded.

"I have been standing too much this past week. Don't worry about me, Clarinda, but if the pain gets worse I may slip away early. My grandson will bring you home."

"I will find you a chair for you as soon as we reach the ballroom," Clarinda murmured.

*

Hetherington House in Park Lane was an old and rambling building that had a charm of its own.

Unlike the other balls which Clarinda had attended there was not one ballroom but four. Two opened out of each other, the others each had their own band.

It was entertaining to roam from one to the other finding a different sort of dance to a different sort of music. It was a novelty that intrigued even the most spoilt and blasé.

The real difficulty at Hetherington House, Clarinda discovered, was to find one's partner. The numerous rooms and winding corridors were so crowded that it was hard to move about.

At the same time Clarinda realised that the floral decorations were unexpectedly lovely and the supper room, decorated like a Moorish tent, was something that she had never seen before.

Her partner after supper had not yet found her and now she was moving along a corridor alone, when she met Lady Romayne Ramsey who was looking, Clarinda thought, even more beautiful than usual. Her dress of ruby-red gauze did little to conceal her sinuous figure and her raven-black hair was a perfect background for an enormous tiara of rubies and diamonds. A ruby necklace glowed against her white neck, the fire of the gems seeming to accentuate the seduction of her eyes.

"Why, Miss Vernon, I was looking for you," she exclaimed on seeing Clarinda.

"Your Ladyship was looking for me," Clarinda asked in surprise.

She was sure that Lady Romayne had a dislike of her because the acknowledged beauty had pointedly ignored her ever since she had arrived at Melburne House.

"Yes, indeed," Lady Romayne replied. "There is an old friend of yours, Miss Vernon, who is anxious to renew your acquaintance. He knew that you were in the supper room and he asked me if I would be obliging enough to bring you to him. I was just on my way to find you."

"I don't think I would have any old friends here," Clarinda said hesitatingly, wondering why Lady Romayne should appear so gushing and so feeling vaguely uncomfortable because she could not understand this sudden change of attitude.

"Now you have become a success you must not forget or ignore those you knew before you came to London," Lady Romayne said admonishingly, "for this friend of yours tells me that he met you in the country."

Clarinda's puzzled expression cleared. Of course she knew who it was. It must be Julien! Julien Wilsdon come to London perhaps on leave from the Army.

She was surprised for a while that he had asked Lady Romayne to find her, then thought that perhaps he was feeling shy in such grand company. She remembered that he had met Lady Romayne and they had talked at The Priory when she had so very foolishly run away.

"I think I know of whom you are speaking," Clarinda said with a smile.

"I thought you might guess," Lady Romayne replied, "but it is supposed to be a surprise, so you must not ask me if your supposition is right or wrong. Come with me, I will take you to him."

She took Clarinda by the hand as she spoke and drew her out of the corridor and down a narrow passage that was marked '*Private*'. Clarinda thought that Lady Romayne must know the Earl and Countess of Hetherington well and therefore had permission, even at such a large party as this, to wander into their private apartments.

The passage, obviously not supposed to be used, was unlit, but Lady Romayne seemed to know the way. At the end of it she opened a door and Clarinda had a quick glance at a small, cosy sitting room such as might be used by a housekeeper or a Governess.

"Thank you, it was kind of you to bring me here," she said to Lady Romayne and entered the room.

For a moment she thought it was empty. Then someone closed the door behind her and she heard the key turn in the lock.

She swung round to become speechless with horror when she saw that it was not Julien who stood smiling at her but Sir Gerald Kean.

CHAPTER TEN

Lady Romayne was not a particularly stupid woman, but she was extremely conceited.

This was not surprising because, having been fêted and acclaimed ever since she left the schoolroom, she had begun to believe that her beauty was a talisman which would procure her anything she wished for anywhere in the world.

Having made up her mind to marry Lord Melburne, she did not credit that his obvious reluctance to ask her to marry him was anything but a childish obstinacy that made him very determined not to surrender his bachelor freedom until he was forced to do so.

She recognised that she attracted him physically and she was convinced that eventually he would come to love her as whole-heartedly and adoringly as all the other men who cast themselves at her feet beseeching her favours.

Because Lord Melburne was so elusive, he attracted her all the more and she made up her mind that sooner or later he must succumb to the prompting of his heart and ask her to be his wife.

She could in a way understand his reluctance to be tied to one woman. His philandering and his many love affairs were public knowledge and Lady Romayne had no illusions about the difficulties she might have in keeping him faithful to her.

At the same time she told herself, with a little shrug of her white shoulders, all that was of little consequence. Once they had been married, he would be fully occupied in keeping importunate suitors away from her and, if very occasionally he glanced at another woman, she would still be the chatelaine of Melburne and the wife who bore his name.

Lady Romayne had lived for too long in the fashionable world to believe that love was anything more than an infatuation of the senses, she knew that the most important factor in marriage was to obtain the right sort of stability in terms of social position and wealth.

Buck Melburne could give her all the things she still craved for in life. She had money of her own, but, although she was at the moment the rage of the young Bucks of St. James's, she was well aware that their acclaim would fade just as quickly as her looks. She wanted to be sure that her husband had both dignity and an unassailable standing in the Social world.

She had, it was true, been perturbed at the news that Nicholas Vernon had brought her of Lord Melburne's betrothal to an unknown girl. But when she saw Clarinda she was at once convinced that there must be a secret reason for this mystifying and unexplained situation.

When nothing more was heard of marriage and Lord Melburne had become Clarinda's Guardian, Lady Romayne told herself that the whole arrangement had something to do with the Priory Estate being adjacent to Melburne and Buck's interest in this country wench could be simply accounted for by the word 'duty'.

Lady Romayne, it was very true, was extremely piqued when Clarinda became a success overnight and was talked of as 'the most beautiful *debutante* of the Season'. But her many informants, and Lady Romayne had many, told her how little interest Lord Melburne showed in his Ward, never dancing with her at the balls, never driving her in his high perch phaeton and never being seen having an intimate conversation with her.

There was also talk of his being interested in a new 'bit of muslin' in the *Corps de Ballet* and of dining twice in one week at the house of one of his old flirts. They were then reported immediately to have resuscitated an affection that everyone thought had ceased to exist.

'No,' Lady Romayne told herself, 'Buck is not interested in that tiresome girl.'

But she did think that the fact that Clarinda was staying in his house, which necessitated his grandmother being his guest, meant that he had less time to spend in her own company than he had done hitherto.

What was obviously important was that Clarinda should get married and so be out of the way. Then, Lady Romayne thought, she would return to her onslaught on Buck's sensibilities in which she was quite convinced that she would be the victor.

As she left Clarinda in the Governess's sitting room at the end of the private passage at Hetherington House, she told herself that she was doing the girl a good turn.

Sir Gerald Kegan might seem sinister to some women as he was undoubtedly extremely wealthy and, if he proposed marriage, which seemed likely, Clarinda might be well advised to accept him.

Anyway it was all up to Sir Gerald to persuade the young chit that he was a desirable husband and, most *debutantes* of Clarinda's age had a partiality for older men.

Lady Romayne was smiling as she left the unlit passage and glanced at the notice reading '*Private*' that was affixed to the wall. It was most unlikely that anyone would disturb them, she thought, and Sir Gerald would doubtless be grateful to her for arranging the *tête-à-tête* for which apparently he had a most ardent desire.

She had always heard that he was extremely generous when it came to gifts for services rendered and wondered whether she might ask him for a large diamond brooch shaped like a butterfly that she had seen in a jeweller's window in Bond Street.

Lady Romayne was greedy for jewels and her lovers, although she was discreet about them, found her insatiably grasping for a tangible expression of their affection.

'Yes,' she decided, 'I shall certainly ask Sir Gerald for the butterfly.'

Then, through the crowd milling backwards and forwards along the corridor, she saw a figure approaching who made her heart leap at once. There was no reason to question why Lord Melburne was called irresistible. He had qualities that made him stand out in an almost startling manner wherever he might appear.

Tonight it was not only the elegance of his evening coat nor the many intricate folds of his snowy-white cravat, it was rather something in the carriage of his head, the breadth of his shoulders and, most of all, the expression on his face.

'Could any man be more handsome and more physically beguiling?' she asked herself.

Almost pushing several people aside she stood in front of Lord Melburne and looked up at him, her eyes very soft and her red lips smiling provocatively.

"Where have you been all evening, Buck?" she asked in the voice that she could make so seductive that every word seemed to have a hidden meaning. "I have been looking for you and longing to see you."

"I have been playing cards, Romayne," Lord Melburne answered. "Let me compliment you. You are in great good looks."

"Come and dance with me," Lady Romayne pleaded.

"I regret I cannot oblige you," he replied, "although I am convinced you have no lack of partners. I am searching for Clarinda."

"I want to dance with you," Lady Romayne protested. "We so seldom see each other these days or if you prefer we could talk together in the garden. There is much I wish to say to you."

"Another time, Romayne," he replied firmly. "At the moment I have a message from my grandmother that I must convey to my Ward."

"You are far too busy playing the anxious nursemaid. It does not become you," Lady Romayne declared. "Come and dance and afterwards I will tell you where she is."

"Tell me first," Lord Melburne replied, "and then I might consider your offer."

There was a touch of sarcasm in his voice.

"Now you are being unkind," Lady Romayne said pouting at him, "so as a punishment I shall not tell you where your Ward is hidden. Besides you have no need to trouble yourself about her, she is being very well amused, I can assure you."

"Who is she with?" Lord Melburne's voice was sharp.

"Someone who I am convinced is making her an offer of marriage. If she accepts, you will be free, Buck, free to give me a little more of your attention than you have done this past month. I know it must have been irksome for you having the responsibility of a girl hardly out of the schoolroom. Soon, I am convinced, your difficulties will be over."

"Who is with Clarinda and where is she?" Lord Melburne demanded impatiently.

"I have told you that she is very pleasantly engaged," Lady Romayne answered. "What woman does not enjoy herself when a man lays his heart at her feet? And you will not be able to find her, Buck, however hard you try, so don't be tiresome. Come and dance with me."

"*Who is with her*?" Lord Melburne demanded and now he spoke fiercely.

The hard and determined tone in his voice made Lady Romayne cry angrily,

"You are being nonsensical about the wench! Leave her alone, I am sure she is enjoying herself far more than we are."

Lady Romayne put out her hand as she spoke and laid it on Lord Melburne's arm.

"Let's talk as we used to do!" she suggested softly and her voice had an almost siren-like seductiveness.

Lord Melburne unexpectedly put out his hand and took Lady Romayne's in his. It was a small well-shaped hand with long tapering fingers.

Lady Romayne had undone part of her white-kid glove and slipped her hand through it. The candlelight shone on the diamonds that encircled her Wedding finger.

"Where is Clarinda?" Lord Melburne repeated.

As they had been talking, they had edged a little out of the crowd and were now standing in the doorway of an anteroom that was empty save for two couples at the far end.

"I am not going to tell you," she replied petulantly. "You are becoming a bore."

She stopped suddenly and gave a cry,

"You are hurting me!"

Lord Melburne was holding her hand in his and now he bent back the first finger slowly but relentlessly.

"Buck, what are you doing? That is painful!"

"I mean it to be," he answered. "Either you tell me where Clarinda is this very moment or I swear to you, Romayne, I will break your finger. It will be extremely uncomfortable for the next few weeks and, swathed in bandages, very unbecoming."

"You are mad!" she spat at him, "quite mad!"

"Merely determined," he answered. "Where is Clarinda?"

For one moment it appeared as if Lady Romayne would defy him, but, as he bent her finger a little further, she gave another cry,

"She is down – the corridor – towards the supper room," she now panted. "It is the first passage – on the right – marked '*Private*' – the room at the end."

"Thank you," Lord Melburne said mockingly.

He turned as he spoke and strode away from her.

She stood looking after him, her face puckered with anger as she rubbed the finger of her left hand, which she fancied was already swollen.

*

Clarinda's astonishment at finding Sir Gerald Kegan in the room that Lady Romayne had taken her to, was only equalled by her feeling of terror as she realised that he had locked the door.

"I t-think – there is some – mistake," she stammered. "I was – e-expecting to find – Mr. Julien Wilsdon here."

"There is no mistake," Sir Gerald answered and she thought that he seemed even more debauched and evil than he had looked that night when he and Nicholas had taken her from The Priory to the caves.

"I have no – wish to talk with – you, sir," Clarinda said, "if that is your – intention."

"I want a great deal more than talk," Sir Gerald replied.

Seeing the expression in his eyes and the sudden smile on his thick lips, Clarinda almost instinctively took a pace back. She was beginning to tremble, but she felt that she must not let him see her fear.

"We have – n-nothing to say to each – other," she said. "I – wish to – forget our last – meeting. Kindly open – the door."

"I have no intention of opening the door until I have been repaid for what you cheated me from attaining that night at the caves."

"I don't – understand," Clarinda stuttered.

"I think you do," he answered. "I am sure you were well aware that I was not going to allow Nicholas Vernon to ravish you after the Mass had been said. I had arranged with Moll that just before the Service had started she would pour into his wine the drug that had been intended for you. I would have taken his place in the Service and when it ended you would have been mine, Clarinda."

"But I – was – rescued," Clarinda faltered.

"Yes, you were rescued," Sir Gerald agreed, "and so you defrauded me of my rights. That is what I am claiming now."

He moved a step towards her as he spoke and again Clarinda retreated.

"Are you – c-crazed?" she asked in a frightened voice. "You cannot behave in – such a manner here in a – private house – at a ball where there are hundreds of people – surely you are – aware that if I – scream someone will come to my – rescue."

"It is extremely unlikely," Sir Gerald answered, "and if you scream too loudly, my dear, I shall have to take somewhat drastic action. I have only to encircle your pretty white neck with my hands and squeeze tightly enough to throttle your voice in your throat. You would be unable to make yourself heard!"

He smiled in a manner that sickened her as she knew that what he was saying excited him.

"It is a slightly painful process," he continued, "for I would not render you unconscious. I don't like making love to women who are unconscious and I also prefer it if they are not speechless."

"You are – insane!" Clarinda cried.

"Not at all. You are Venus, the sacrifice to Satan of a pure untouched virgin. I promised myself that I would be your Master, your instructor in the joys of love and I do *not* intend to be defrauded of that joy."

"How can you speak of love when it is part of the wickedness and blasphemy that you and Nicholas indulged in?" Clarinda asked angrily. "What I saw of the – degradation and – licentiousness taking place in the caves, it made me ashamed that men who were presumed to be gentlemen – educated and civilised – should lower themselves to behave like beasts."

Sir Gerald laughed.

"You are lovely when you are incensed, Clarinda, and you have courage! You behaved with great bravery when Nicholas and I took you to the caves. You will need that same virtue now, for I intend to make you mine and I promise you there is no escape."

There was something infinitely menacing in the pleasantness of his tone. He made no movement but Clarinda felt as if he had come nearer and was already reaching out his arms towards her.

With a superhuman effort, she put up her chin and said,

"I appeal to you, sir, to behave – decently – I cannot believe that what you are saying is – not just mere talk to – frighten me. No gentleman who has any semblance of honour could stoop to – insult a woman who is – defenceless. Let me go, I beg of you and we will forget that this – conversation has ever occurred."

"Well done," he applauded. "You are more valiant, my dear, than any woman I have ever met. But it will avail you nothing, for I desire you and you attract me as no Venus has ever done before."

His eyes flickered over her body.

"It is such a pity," he went on, "that the Service could not have proceeded as had been intended. I grant you that Melburne was clever in snatching you away under our very noses, but Melburne is not here now and the door is locked. Come, Clarinda, and concede you are beaten, for

I swear to you there is no escape. Look at me and you will see that it is the truth."

Because she was so frightened she obeyed him and found herself looking into his eyes, dark lustful eyes that seemed to have a frightening fire smouldering in their depths, eyes that were staring at her in a manner that not only made her feel shy but ashamed, as if she stood naked before him.

Suddenly she felt that his eyes were getting bigger, larger and more compelling.

"Come to me, Clarinda," he said softly. "*Come to me.*"

His voice was hardly above a whisper, but she felt as if it vibrated through her very body.

Then suddenly she realised what was happening. She was moving towards him, going to him as he commanded, held by his eyes, eyes that she could not wrench away her own from. He was hypnotising her. She knew it, even as in a panic she realised that she could not resist him.

Then, even as she felt a darkness enveloping her, she began to pray,

'Help me, God – *please help me.*'

It was the same prayer she had repeated over and over again in the caves. It had saved her then and it had brought Lord Melburne to her rescue.

'Help me, God – help me.'

As if the prayer released her from Sir Gerald's evil magnetism, she found that she could turn her eyes away from his and in that moment she was free of them.

She ran across the room, putting the sofa between herself and him. She stood holding on to the back of it, her fingers biting into the soft damask while she trembled with a terror that seemed to shake her whole body.

Sir Gerald laughed. It was a laugh of a man who is intrigued and sexually excited, a man who knows he had the object of his desire well within his grasp.

He moved slowly towards her, his eyes on her face, and she knew that she had thrilled him by her resistance and it was useless to beg for his mercy. She could only try to escape and attempt to fight him.

He approached the sofa and Clarinda made herself ready to run from whichever way he came to her.

"Come, Clarinda," he said, "you cannot evade me for long. It is only a question of time before I hold you in my arms. You are like a little bird caught in a net. You can flutter and struggle but you cannot fly away."

"Leave me – alone!" Clarinda cried desperately.

"Do you think I could ever forget you as Venus?" he asked. "The whiteness of your body beneath the transparency of your robe. Your figure is delectable, my dear, and the softness of your mouth will be more delectable still. I want you, Clarinda, and what I want I take!"

He made as if to come behind the sofa and, as she began to run from him, he changed his direction and, reaching out his long arms, caught her.

She gave a scream as he pulled her roughly against his chest. And then his mouth was on hers, suffocating her cries, giving her such a feeling of disgust beyond expression and which seemed to take even her breath away from her.

She felt that his thick lips, hard, brutal and possessive, dragged her down to the slimy depths of some filth from which she could never be clean again. She tried to fight against him but it was impossible. His mouth held her completely and absolutely captive and she could not even struggle within his enveloping arms.

Then she felt him move her a little to the right before he tumbled her backwards onto the sofa. She gave a shrill cry as she fell down against the softness of the cushions and felt him throw his whole weight upon her.

She screamed and once more his lips were on hers. Her hands fluttered ineffectually as a moth's as she struck at him and tried to push him away.

She knew with a kind of dazed horror that his desire for her prevented his being aware of anything save the evil passion that now enflamed him to the point where he was oblivious of everything but his own lust.

She felt his hand tearing at her breast and ripping away the soft gauze of her gown. Then despairingly, as she knew she must die of the horror of what he was about to do, she heard a sudden crash.

Just for a moment Sir Gerald seemed to stiffen, although he did not lift his mouth from her lips. The crash came again and this time the door flew open as the wood splintered away from the lock.

Sir Gerald raised his head and, as Lord Melburne advanced across the room towards him, he raised himself from off Clarinda's body.

For one moment the two men faced each other before Lord Melburne hit Sir Gerald hard in the face with his clenched fist. It was the blow of a man who had learnt his boxing from Masters of the art.

Sir Gerald staggered and Lord Melburne hit him again and this time he collapsed against the further end of the sofa.

"How dare you strike me!" Sir Gerald shouted out at him furiously. "If you want a fight, Melburne – "

"I fight with gentlemen not vermin," Lord Melburne replied and hit him again.

Sir Gerald was a heavy man and no coward. He struggled to his feet, but Lord Melburne was like an avenging angel and both his fists smashed into his face.

Sir Gerald staggered against the fireplace and, picking up a heavy poker, he advanced towards Lord Melburne, holding the weapon high, the snarl of a cornered wild beast upon his lips.

With lithe dexterity, Lord Melburne avoided the blow from the poker and he then gave Sir Gerald an uppercut under the chin with his right hand, which lifted him almost from the ground.

He hit him again with his left and again and yet again, driving him backwards until he collapsed against the wall of the room to slither slowly down onto the floor, his legs stretched out in front of him and his head falling sideways onto his shoulder.

He was bleeding from his nose and his mouth and both his eyes were partially closed.

Lord Melburne stood looking down at him, his fists still clenched, an expression of fury contorting his face.

"Get up, you *damned* swine," he called out, "I have not finished with you yet."

But Sir Gerald was incapable of moving. Lord Melburne glanced around and on a nearby table was a large vase of roses. He threw the roses on the table and flung the water in the vase into Sir Gerald's face.

For a moment it seemed as if the douche had no effect.

Then Sir Gerald's eyes opened slowly.

"Can you hear me?" Lord Melburne bellowed, "Then listen carefully. If you are not out of this country in forty-eight hours, never to return, I will have you arrested. I have irrefutable proof that you financed and decorated the Hell Fire Caves on the Vernon Estate. I have not acted on this before because Miss Vernon might have been involved in the disclosure of your filthy practices. But now her name need not be mentioned and I can use the evidence I have collected and I will use it convincingly."

Lord Melburne paused and, before speaking more slowly and even clearer, he went on,

"You will also be charged with being an accessory to the murder of a child of a month old whose mother swears that it was sacrificed in the caves. The corpse of the baby has been discovered buried in the field just outside the caves themselves and will be produced in the case that has been prepared against you. You know the penalty if you are found guilty, which you will be."

Lord Melburne looked down at Sir Gerald with both scorn and disgust in his expression.

"You deserve to hang," he thundered, "but I give you one chance. You have forty-eight hours to leave England for ever. If you return, there will be a warrant waiting for you."

Lord Melburne paused for a moment as if he expected Sir Gerald to reply, but the beaten man's eyes closed wearily and he slithered still lower onto the floor until he was lying nearly full-length.

It was then that Lord Melburne turned towards Clarinda. She was sitting up on the sofa, her eyes wide and frightened although she was not crying. Her hands were clasped over her torn dress and it seemed to Lord Melburne that she was almost afraid to move, as if she was caught in some terrible nightmare that she could not awake from.

He put out his hand and drew her to her feet.

"Come, Clarinda, I will take you home."

"Y-yes," she whispered, almost beneath her breath, "please – t-take – me home."

He saw that her torn gown could not be hidden and he looked around the room.

On the back of a chair there was a small embroidered shawl with a long fringe. He then picked it up, folded it in a triangle and put it around Clarinda's shoulders.

She said nothing but crossed it over her breasts with trembling hands. Then with his arm under hers he led her out of the room, down the unlit passage and into the corridor still filled with people moving to and from the supper room.

They walked quickly and, although people tried to speak to Lord Melburne, he ignored them. They reached the front door and asked for his carriage.

Only as they drove away did Clarinda give an almost inarticulate murmur and, putting out her hand, she held onto his in an almost frantic grip.

"I am – so frightened," she muttered.

Her voice held a terror in it that was past tears and then his fingers closed tightly over hers.

"We will talk when we are at home," he replied soothingly. "You have had a bad shock, Clarinda, but it is over now and he will never trouble you again, I promise you."

She did not reply and they drove in silence. It was not far from Park Lane to Berkeley Square and Lord Melburne's fine horses travelled the distance in a very short space of time.

Lord Melburne helped Clarinda from the carriage and, holding her arm in his, he drew her across the hall and into the library.

He refused the attentions of the servants and fetched her a small glass of brandy.

"I don't – need – it," she tried to say but, looking up at his face and realising that he was determined she should drink it, without further argument she raised the glass to her lips.

She felt the fiery spirit seep down her throat. It made her choke, but she knew that at the same time it took away some of the ice-cold fear that seemed to lie like a heavy stone in her breast.

"No – more – please," she pleaded and gave him back the glass half-full.

"I am sorry, Clarinda, that this should have happened," Lord Melburne said. "But Kegan will leave the country. He will not risk prosecution."

"You – don't – understand," Clarinda trembled, clasping her hands together.

"What do I not understand?" Lord Melburne asked gently.

She seemed to find it hard to find words to answer him. Her face was very pale, her eyes dark pools of pain.

It appeared to him that she was beyond tears and in the grip of a fear that made him remember the faces of men he had seen under fire for the first time.

There had been the same expression of shock in their eyes that he saw now in Clarinda's when they had seen a comrade die beside them. Lord Melburne felt he must say something to comfort her, to reassure her and to take away her strained desperate look.

"You are safe, Clarinda," he said. "You will never see him again. You can believe me, I swear I will protect you from him."

"But you – cannot – protect me from the – others," Clarinda whimpered.

For a moment he could not follow who she meant.

"The others?" he questioned.

"The masked men – in the – caves. Do you not understand – I was Venus – the sacrifice they had been – promised, that is what – Sir Gerald – wanted of me tonight – the Venus of whom he had been – defrauded."

For the first time she gave a little sob.

"They will be – waiting for – me, I cannot – escape them – wherever I go I shall be – afraid, for I don't – know who they are. I have never seen – them without their masks."

Lord Melburne drew a deep breath. Then he sat down beside Clarinda on the sofa taking both her hands in his firm grasp.

"Listen to me, Clarinda. I know now what you are so afraid of and I do understand. But fortunately there is an answer to your fear. A very simple one."

She looked up at him and he felt that there was a sudden flicker of hope in her eyes.

"It is this," Lord Melburne went on. "What these men are seeking, if indeed they are all as bestial as Kegan, which I doubt, is Venus, the pure untouched virgin, who is the sacrifice to Satan. Once you are married they will no longer have any interest in you. It is not only your husband who will protect you from them but the fact that you are no longer eligible to play the part of Venus. Do you see?"

She gave a deep sigh and he felt her fingers tighten on his.

Then she said in an almost childish voice and one that no longer held the frantic terror that had possessed her before,

"But I – have – no husband."

"That is surely something that can quite easily be remedied," Lord Melburne suggested.

Her fingers slackened on his and he realised that, after what she had been through, she was almost on the point of collapse.

"Go to bed, Clarinda," he said softly. "You are safe here in this house, as you well know. My room is not very far away from yours. I will leave my door open just in case you should call out and feel afraid, but you know as well as I do that no one would disturb you. You are completely safe for tonight and tomorrow we can talk of this further and we can make plans."

"I cannot – go to another – ball," Clarinda cried, "I cannot – go – anywhere I might meet – men like – him."

"Shall we go to the country?" Lord Melburne asked.

"To The Priory?"

He knew by the tone of her voice that the thought of The Priory frightened her as well.

"To Melburne," he answered.

"Could we – really?" she asked and life seemed to come back into her face bringing with it a faint touch of colour.

"There is nothing to prevent us. I will talk to Grandmama in the morning and we can be there before luncheon. Will that please you?"

"If only we – could go – tonight," she whispered.

"I think that would be rather unkind to my grandmother," he said. "I was looking for you at the ball, Clarinda, to tell you that she had gone home early. Her rheumatism was hurting her and I would not wish to disturb her now if she is asleep."

"No, no, it was – selfish of – me to think of it," Clarinda admitted.

"Would you like Betty to sleep in your room?" he enquired.

She shook her head.

"No, I am being – nonsensical – I don't wish to tell Betty what has happened – I don't want to – talk about it to – anyone."

"There is no reason why you should. Let me help you upstairs to bed."

"No, no, I am not – ill," she answered. "I am just – being foolish, but – "

She looked up at him a little piteously.

"You will leave your door – open?"

"I have given you my word," he replied, "and you know well that no one would dare to frighten you while I am here."

He walked with her to the door.

"Good night, Clarinda," he said very gently. "Sleep well and don't be afraid. Things will seem better in the morning and we will find a solution together, that I do promise you."

She made a valiant effort at a smile and dropped him a curtsey. It was a very low curtsey as if she thanked him by the reverence of it and as she rose she unexpectedly reached out and took his hand in hers.

His knuckles were bruised and bleeding from the violent way that he had hit Sir Gerald. She pressed her lips against them and, as he looked down at her with a darkness in his eyes, which she would not have understood, she opened the door and slipped away.

*

The Dowager was breakfasting in her room at seven of the clock the following morning when there came a tap at the door.

She looked up with an expression of irritation on her face, because she liked to be alone at breakfast. She had long ago decided that, as her rheumatism was at its worst when she first woke, she would see no one until she was in less pain and felt more genial towards the world in general.

"Come in," she called grudgingly and was astonished as the door opened to reveal, not one of the senior servants as she had expected, but her grandson, dressed with an elegance that always pleased her eye.

She noticed, however, that he looked tired and there were dark circles under his eyes as if he had been awake all night. This surprised her since she had heard him return home with Clarinda quite early.

"Good morning, Grandmama," Lord Melburne greeted her.

You are very early, Buck," the Dowager exclaimed, "I had no idea I was to be honoured by your presence at breakfast!"

"I have already had mine," Lord Melburne replied, "and I know, Grandmama, that you like to be alone at cockcrow. But I particularly wish to speak with you."

"It must be a matter of tremendous import to bring you from the comfort of your bed at such an unfashionable hour unless you are going to a mill are departing for the races," the Dowager commented.

"I am doing neither. We are leaving at about half after ten this morning for Melburne and I thought, ma'am, that you would desire plenty of time to prepare yourself."

"And you call that plenty of time?" the Dowager smiled. "Why this sudden decision?"

Lord Melburne looked away from her and she realised that he was choosing his words with care.

"Something happened last night that upset Clarinda," he replied. "She has no wish at the moment to attend any further balls or entertainments. There is a decision to be made and it must be made in the country."

"I would suppose she has decided to accept one of those lovelorn swains who have been mooning around the house all these past weeks," the Dowager remarked. "Is it likely to be the Duke?"

Lord Melburne shook his head.

"No, Grandmama, I regret I must disappoint you, but it will not be the Duke."

"Then I will make no further guesses. I suppose you have some good reason for taking Clarinda away when she is at the height of her success, when she is acclaimed not only as the most beautiful *debutante* there has been for an age but also the most charming and the best-mannered with, of course, the exception of her extraordinary behaviour yesterday afternoon at Devonshire House."

"His Grace was somewhat overpowering," Lord Melburne explained.

"It is such a pity – " the Dowager began, but a glance at her grandson's face checked the words before she could utter them.

She had not seen that bleak look in his eyes since the death of his mother whom he had adored. There was that same blue line round his mouth which had made her both then and now long to put her arms round him and hold him close.

"What is amiss, Buck?" she enquired gently.

"I hope," he said slowly in a voice deliberately devoid of feeling, "I can settle Clarinda's affairs for her within the next few days and then, Grandmama, I intend to go abroad."

"Go abroad!" the Dowager repeated, her voice rising. "Why in Heaven's name should you wish to go abroad?"

"I have a great desire to see Paris again and perhaps Rome."

"Fustian!" his grandmother exclaimed. "You know I am not likely to be fobbed off by such moonshine! What is the real reason?"

"Don't be too perceptive, Grandmama," Lord Melburne pleaded. "Don't try to probe too deeply. It is just that I have no wish to stay here once Clarinda's future has been arranged."

"Well, I hope that indeed you will be able to settle it to her satisfaction," the Dowager said. "It always distresses me to see someone as pretty as Clarinda so unhappily in love."

"In love!" Lord Melburne expostulated. "Who said Clarinda was in love?"

"But, of course, she is in love," the Dowager snapped. "Do you imagine, my dear Buck, that girls who are not in love go around refusing great matrimonial catches like the Duke of Kingston or spend half the night sobbing into their pillows."

"Clarinda has been crying? I knew she was upset last night – "

"I have no idea what Clarinda did last night," the Dowager continued, "but Betty tells me that almost every night her pillow is wet with tears and that she cries uncontrollably when she is alone. Women cry, Buck, when their hearts are aching for a man!"

"But for whom could she be crying?" Lord Melburne asked in bewilderment.

"I thought that you would be the most likely to know the answer to that question," the Dowager reproved him "It certainly cannot be any of the gentlemen who have offered for her not once but a dozen times. If you have had some of them pleading with you for help, I assure you I have had twice as many begging my co-operation in making her accept them."

"Blast it! But then who in God's name can it be?" Lord Melburne asked angrily, as if the mystery was incensing him to the point of losing his self-control.

"I will excuse your language," the Dowager said coldly, "because I infer you are really concerned about Clarinda's happiness. Betty is persuaded that it is a man the child knew in the country."

"That is just impossible!" Lord Melburne retorted. "The only men she knew were Julien Wilsdon, who is a mere boy not much older than herself, Nicholas Vernon, who is now dead, and – "

He stopped suddenly, an almost stupefied look on his face as if a sudden idea had come to him. An idea so unexpected and so revolutionary, that he sat still and rigid as if turned to stone.

The Dowager said nothing, watching him with her shrewd bright eyes, till suddenly as if galvanised into action he rose to his feet and she knew that their conversation was at an end.

"Your servant, Grandmama," he said. "I hope you can be ready by ten-thirty. Clarinda will travel with you in your carriage. I shall drive my phaeton."

"I will be ready," she replied, "and I hope that this hasty departure from London, which I deprecate, will at least solve the problem of Clarinda's tears."

"I earnestly hope so, ma'am," Lord Melburne concurred.

She saw a sudden glint in his eyes like a leaping flame, which was in strange contrast to the solemnity of his voice. The blue look had gone from his mouth.

He left closing the door behind him and, when she was alone, the Dowager gave a little chuckle as if she was extremely amused by some private joke.

CHAPTER ELEVEN

Clarinda galloped down Dingle's Ride and found it a joy to be mounted on a horse again, especially one from Lord Melburne's perfect stables.

She had slipped away when luncheon was over, feeling strongly that she must be alone and determined to tell no one where she was going.

She wanted to visit The Priory and, although she was sure that neither the Dowager nor Lord Melburne would wish to accompany her, she had a slight feeling of guilt because she had not told them of her plans.

She had spent a sleepless night after she had left Lord Melburne in the library. She had tossed and turned, living over and over those extreme moments of horror and humiliation when she had been unable to escape from Sir Gerald and had felt herself helpless beneath him.

Now it seemed as clearly as if he was by her side, that she could hear Lord Melburne's voice telling her that the only way she could be safe and the only way she could avoid the menaces of the masked men who had seen her in the role of Venus, was to marry!

She drew up her horse at the end of Dingle's Ride and recalled the wild elation of the morning when she tried to escape from Lord Melburne and he had outridden her on Saladin, his stallion with Arab blood in it.

She had hated him, but there had been something stimulating and thrilling in her very defiance of him.

As she thought of it, she turned her horse across the Ride and rode on down the twisting path through the wood that led into the lush green parkland which surrounded The Priory.

There was the sweet fresh smell of the countryside that she had so missed in London, the trees full-leaved and the hedgerows thick with wild roses and honeysuckle.

But Clarinda was recalling her feelings when she had ridden away from Lord Melburne after he had proved himself the victor in Dingle's Ride.

Her hatred had been unmixed and bitter. It was a violent hatred for the man who she had loathed for over four years because of the way that he had treated her friend, Jessica Tansley. There had been no complications or compromise then about her emotions.

It must have been after Lord Melburne had rescued her from the caves, Clarinda thought, that she had found that it was becoming difficult to go on nourishing her anger against him. Perhaps it had begun even earlier than that, maybe it was that moment when he had shaken her and fiercely kissed her mouth because he had seen her embracing Julien Wilsdon.

She had never been able to forget the touch of his lips, at first hard and almost cruel in their pressure on hers and then suddenly persuading, beguiling and possessive as if they will draw her very heart from her breast.

She remembered how she had meant to remain icily calm and rigid within his arms, but because his kisses had disturbed her beyond endurance, she had flared out at him, incensed with a fear not so much of him as of herself.

Clarinda gave a little sob.

"Oh, God," she said cried out aloud, "why did this have to happen to me?"

She had cried last night into her pillow as she had cried so many nights before, not only because she felt helpless and vulnerable and afraid but because she knew that however great a success she might be in the Social world, she could never find happiness with any of the men who had besought her so ardently to marry them.

How could she possibly marry anyone when her affections were captured hopelessly and irrevocably by a man for whom, she told herself, she had no respect and who did not love her anyway?

She had loved Lord Melburne before they went to London. But, when he appeared to ignore her, had contrived never to be alone with her and had never asked her to dance at any of the balls which they attended, she had to acknowledge that there was an aching emptiness within her which no amount of praise and adulation from other men could dispense.

She had fought against such a betrayal of her friend, accusing herself night after night of disloyalty, of hypocrisy and of being weak and vacillating.

Yet however much she condemned herself and however much she flagellated herself with reproaches, the fact remained that she only had to see Lord Melburne's broad shoulders coming towards her at some party, to have a glimpse of him ascending the stairs at Melburne House and to watch him seated at the end of his dining table for her heart to turn over in her breast.

She would feel a strange breathless thrill running through her that was unmistakably and irrefutably *love*!

'Don't let me love him, please God, don't let me love him,' she had prayed, knowing, even as she said the words in the darkness of her bedchamber, that it was too late!

She knew now that she had loved him when he had come to her rescue in the caves and she had loved him when he had held her racked with tears in his strong arms. She had loved him as she pleaded with him not to leave her after he had carried her upstairs to lay her gently on her bed!

Yet now she had to marry someone else. She had to choose a husband from one of her many suitors, while her own heart was irretrievably given for ever to a man who was not in the least interested in her.

Perhaps, Clarinda thought despairingly, that if she had behaved differently he might have been attracted by her.

Then she remembered that all the women in whom he had been interested had been dark-haired. There was Lady Romayne with her raven-black elegantly coiffured locks, there was Liane, who Betty had told her was French and who was dark-haired.

And there were various other lovely women who she suspected of being old flirts of Lord Melburne because of the way they had looked at her with malice and envy in their eyes and because the Dowager had hinted more or less inadvertently that once they had been in Lord Melburne's life. They were all brunettes,!

Last night Clarinda had fallen asleep from sheer exhaustion just before dawn to have a nightmare that she was in Sir Gerald Kegan's arms and all around them there were masked men jeering and laughing at her helplessness.

She had woken with a muffled cry to find herself trembling and, because the dream had been so vivid, she had slipped out of bed in the dark and opened the door into the passage.

The candles had guttered down low in their silver sconces, but at the end of the landing from which the main bedrooms opened, she could see Lord Melburne's room. His door was ajar and the room was lit inside so that she knew that he was awake and watching over her as he had promised to do.

She felt her fears vanish. She closed her door very quietly and slipped back into bed to lie thinking about him and just how much and hopelessly she loved him until finally for the second time that night she cried bitterly and despairingly.

If the Dowager had noticed the lines under her eyes and her pale face when they left the house for the country, she made no comment.

Clarinda had learnt that Lord Melburne had already gone ahead of them. She wished that she could have driven with him in his high perch phaeton, feeling the wind in her face and, knowing that even if he had no need of her, he was for the moment at her side.

'I love him,' she murmured to herself and knew that she was consumed by an urgency to reach Melburne and see him again.

Now, riding towards The Priory, Clarinda wondered if she would ever be free of the pain which the mere thought of him evoked in her. It was almost like being stabbed by a knife, but at times there was a strange ecstasy in it, because the hurt, agonising though it was, seemed only to intensify her love for him.

Clarinda was so deep in her thoughts that she was well within sight of The Priory itself before she realised it. The long low Elizabethan house, half-hidden by trees and the pointed gables and worn red brick held a familiar beauty which told her that she was now home.

Yet she found herself reining her horse in. She had a sudden irrepressible impulse to turn back to Melburne and not to visit the house she had lived in for four years.

She realised now how restricted her life at The Priory had been. It was Lord Melburne who had compelled her to go to London, who had insisted that she broaden her horizon, that she must meet people and that she must have a chance to shine in London Society.

He had been right, she thought, but then he was always right! She had enjoyed London, even though she had been puzzled and saddened by his indifference to her from the moment they reached Melburne House in Berkeley Square.

However, she would not have been human had she not enjoyed finding out that she was beautiful, that men lost their hearts to her and that even women acclaimed her a huge success.

But now Clarinda knew that she had to face facts. Life would be impossible unless she could find herself a husband! She could never live in peace in the obscurity of The Priory for fear that one of those masked men, knowing who she was, would come in search of her.

She could not go back to London and attend balls because every time a man asked her for a dance she would wonder if he was one of those who had seen her as Venus in the caves.

Even Lord Melburne could not protect her against such a terror as that.

Clarinda reached the drive and walked her horse through a tunnel of green leaves formed by the great oaks.

Everything, she felt bitterly, reminded her of Lord Melburne. Even here she was haunted by her first sight of him tooling his high perch phaeton and looking so incredibly handsome with his high hat sported at a raffish angle and his cravat looking spotlessly white against his sunburnt face.

'I might have known then I would come to love him,' Clarinda told herself with a sob.

If only she had forgotten her hatred and had greeted him pleasantly, perhaps the whole story of their tempestuous relationship might have been different.

'Why did I not say I would be friends with him when he asked me?' she chided herself.

She knew that, although she had told Lord Melburne that the memory of Jessica Tansley lay between them, it was also because she was afraid that if they had any more intimate talks together he would guess that she loved him.

That was an ultimate humiliation that she could not endure.

She could not allow him to guess that she had succumbed to his attractions like all the other women he knew had succumbed. He was the irresistible Buck Melburne, the man who attracted women to the point where they cast away all dignity and discretion and behaved like Lady Romayne, with her air of possessiveness, the provocative pouting of her lips and her hands going out to touch him.

Clarinda felt herself shiver.

'I will not think about him – I will not,' she urged herself.

But now, try as she might, his face was always before her eyes.

She arrived at the big nail-studded oak door of The Priory, which had stood there since the house was first built and found to her surprise that it was open. Old Ned, the ostler, came hurrying to hold her horse and Bates appeared in the doorway.

"Welcome home, Miss Clarinda," he bowed.

"Were you expecting me?" Clarinda asked in surprise.

"Yes, indeed, miss. His Lordship stopped by on his way to Melburne this morning and told us you would be coming sometime today. It's real glad we are to see you, Miss Clarinda, and looking more beautiful, if you'll pardon me for saying so, than I've ever seen you."

Clarinda now realised with a smile that Bates had never before beheld her dressed in a fashionable velvet habit or with her hair arranged skilfully under a high-crowned hat with a floating green veil.

"I am so glad to be here," she answered. "Is everything all right?"

"Everything, Miss Clarinda. We've been putting flowers in the rooms so you wouldn't feel they look as empty-like."

"Thank you, Bates," Clarinda smiled.

She walked across the hall into the salon. She had forgotten how small and low-ceilinged it was and knew that she was comparing it with Melburne. She also noticed the worn covers and threadbare carpets.

If she came to live here, the furnishings of the house would have to be replaced in almost every room! At the thought of it she felt a sudden constriction in her throat.

How could she live here alone? Or even with a husband?

And who would he be?

She walked from the salon and in to the study where her uncle had always sat. She could remember reading aloud to him the books he enjoyed and the long evenings when, tired out and ill, he had slept in the big armchair and she had read to herself. She had not realised how lonely she was and how ignorant of any other life outside the peace and quiet of The Priory.

"What am I to do in the future?" Clarinda asked aloud.

She went to the window to look out on the Rose Garden and to remember how Julien had put his cheek against hers as he was so unhappy and she had then run away because Lord Melburne had seen them.

'What am I to do?' she asked again.

She heard the door open behind her and thought that it must be Bates bringing her some refreshment.

Then she heard his voice announce,

"Lady McDougall, Miss Clarinda."

Clarinda turned round in surprise until, after just one astonished glance at a vision in blue taffeta and blue floating plumes on a high-crowned bonnet, she gave a cry of recognition,

"Jessica! What are you doing here?"

"I thought you might be surprised to see me," the vision answered, "but I was passing the very gates on my way to London and felt that I must call on you."

"It is such a surprise!" Clarinda exclaimed, kissing Jessica's cheek and noticing, while she was still very pretty with her dark hair and slanting eyes, that she was rather plumper and certainly looked older.

"You are married?" she questioned.

Jessica sat down elegantly on the sofa.

"I have been married for over three years," she replied. "I should have written to you, Clarinda. It was remiss of me, but my husband, Sir Fingall McDougall, lives in Scotland and we were married in a great hurry because he desired to return North quickly. So I did not ask you to the Wedding. I suppose you did not read about it in *The Ladies' Journal*?"

"No, indeed! Uncle Roderick did not have anything so frivolous in the house," Clarinda replied with a smile.

"My relations, whom I have been visiting, tell me that your uncle is dead. I am so sorry, dearest, it must have been sad for you. But you look very smart. Are you still living here?"

"No, not at the moment," Clarinda answered.

Then, not looking at her friend, she said a little hesitatingly,

"I am staying at – Melburne. You know it – marches with this estate – Uncle Roderick made – Lord Melburne my – Guardian."

"Your Guardian!" Jessica exclaimed. "Goodness, Clarinda, you are a lucky girl! I cannot imagine anything more exciting. I used to admire Lord Melburne so much. He was just so handsome and so outstanding. I always longed to meet him."

There was a moment's pregnant silence and Clarinda was very still.

"I don't – think you heard me – correctly, Jessica. It is – Lord Melburne who is now my – Guardian."

"I heard you clearly," Jessica smiled. "The Irresistible Buck Melburne! How I longed to make his acquaintance when I was a *debutante*."

Clarinda drew a deep breath.

"But Jessica, you told me – that he had made love to you and – when you – pleaded with him to – marry you, he refused! You told me – every detail. You told me – how much you – loved him and that he – r-ravished you against your will."

Jessica McDougall threw back her head and laughed.

"And you believed all that fustian! Funny little Clarinda! I remember now, telling you all sorts of nonsensical tales while you sat wide-eyed on my bed, believing every word of them. I used to make up all those stories about every attractive man I met or, as in the case of Lord Melburne, whom I did not meet. But I saw him at balls and thought him devastatingly good-looking."

"You mean that – what you told me was not – true?" Clarinda asked stupidly.

"No, of course it was not true!" Jessica exclaimed. "How could you possibly credit such nonsense? But indeed, if you believed me, I must have told my story well, I always fancied, if I had been born in another walk of life, I would have made my fortune on the stage."

"I think you – would," Clarinda whispered.

She rose as she spoke and stood for a moment holding onto the back of a chair. She felt that she must hold onto something.

"Fancy you being a Ward of Lord Melburne," Jessica remarked reflectively. "Well, all I can say, Clarinda, is that you are extremely fortunate to move with the *Bon Ton*. If I was not in such a hurry to reach London, I would ask you to introduce me to his Lordship, but it will not be long before we meet because I have already promised to come South for his marriage."

"His – marriage?" Clarinda echoed.

"Yes, indeed," Jessica replied. "On my way through London I did stay for a night with Lady Romayne Ramsey, she is a relative of my husband's, and she told me that there had been an understanding between her and Lord Melburne for quite some time and they are to be married later on in the summer. I shall see you there and we then must have a long gossip, Clarinda. At the moment I cannot linger."

"You must – go?" Clarinda asked, hardly knowing what she was saying.

"Yes, there is a party being given for me in London tonight and I am so much looking forward to it."

"But will you not – stay and have some – refreshment?" Clarinda enquired.

Her voice sounded strained and seemed to come from a very far distance.

"No, thank you, dearest," Jessica replied. "I had luncheon with some friends a little over an hour ago and I must now be on my way."

She held Clarinda in a close embrace. There was a rustle of silk, an exotic fragrance and the softness of a powdered cheek, then as she moved towards the door she was talking all the time, chattering of her children, her husband, her journey to Scotland and her many friends in London. It was almost impossible to take in what she was saying before she had driven away.

Clarinda stood watching her go as if in a dream. She could never remember afterwards leaving The Priory, she only found herself riding back to Melburne in a daze and feeling that her brain would not work properly.

She reached the great house, left her horse at the stables and went upstairs through one of the side doors.

Once in her bedroom she rang for Betty.

"Did you have a nice ride – ?" Betty asked and then stopped. "What has happened, Miss Clarinda? You look as if you have seen a ghost!"

"I am all – right," Clarinda answered.

"Let me get you some brandy, miss. What can have occurred? You were pale enough this mornin' in all conscience, but now you look worse. You must lie down. You must rest. It's been too much for you, all of this junketin' every night in London and now drivin' off to The Priory. There are things there I don't want to remember and that's a fact."

Clarinda hardly heard a word she said. Only when Betty tried to make her lie down did she rebel.

"I have to go downstairs," she insisted. "I have to see Lord Melburne."

There was so much determination in her voice that Betty said no more. She fetched one of Clarinda's prettiest gowns from the wardrobe, helped her into it and then arranged her hair in the fashionable manner that had captivated London Society.

Clarinda was as placid as a doll beneath her hands. Only when Betty had finished did she turn away from the mirror that she had been staring into with sightless eyes, to walk slowly down the stairs, conscious that her heart was beating frantically and her hands were cold.

Now she felt instinctively that Lord Melburne would be in the library and, as the door was opened for her, she saw that her supposition was right for he was seated at the big flat-topped desk in the centre of the room.

She stood for a moment just inside the door.

Then in a voice, which to her own ears seemed quite steady, she began,

"I wish to speak with your Lordship – if it is – convenient."

"It is indeed, Clarinda," Lord Melburne answered.

He sanded the paper that he had been writing on and then rose to his feet.

"I was about to send for you as it happens. I have something to tell you, Clarinda. I have resigned from being your Guardian."

"You have resigned?" Clarinda exclaimed.

"Yes," he replied. "I have no wish to continue in such a position."

She felt a stab of intolerable pain, knowing that it was because he intended to rid himself of all his responsibility for her. It was not surprising, if he was to be married, that he had no desire to complicate his life any longer with her affairs after all the trouble she had given him in these past weeks.

Then, as he realised that she had not spoken and perhaps sensing her agitation, he said,

"Your pardon, Clarinda, you wished to speak with me. I should have let you do so first."

She came further into the room to stand by the fireplace, twisting her fingers together and looking almost blindly at the long rows of brightly bound books and at the huge vase of hothouse flowers that stood on a table in front of them.

"You had something to say to me," Lord Melburne prompted and his tone was curious.

"Y-yes," Clarinda murmured.

"Will you not begin and shall we not sit down? It would be more comfortable."

"I w-would – rather – stand," Clarinda answered. "I have to – a-apologise to you – my Lord."

"Again?" he asked with a little twist of his lips.

"This time it is much – worse than – anything for – I have had to – apologise for before," Clarinda said.

"Worse?" he asked.

"Much – much – worse."

"What can have happened, I wonder?" he asked. "We have not been here at Melburne for more than a few hours."

"I have been to The – Priory."

"It has upset you?" his voice was sharp.

"Not The – Priory," Clarinda answered, "but – Jessica Tansley called on me – while I was there."

She realised that Lord Melburne was suddenly still.

"Jessica Tansley!"

"She is now – Lady McDougall. She was – passing the – gates."

There was what seemed to Clarinda a terrifying silence that she could not break. She knew that Lord Melburne was waiting for her to continue, but she could not find the words.

Then suddenly they burst from her lips,

"She said that – she had – never met you!"

"I told you that I had never met her," Lord Melburne replied.

"I did not – believe you. How could I – know that she – made it all up? She cried and she told me how she had – pleaded with you – going down on her – knees, begging you to marry her and you – laughed. She made it sound so real – I believed her – of course, I believed her!"

"And may I ask now what I was supposed to have done?" Lord Melburne enquired.

"She – said that you had – r-ravished her," Clarinda answered in a voice hardly above a whisper.

"And you believed her? And how dare you think such things of me? How dare you insult me? Do you think that I have no honour, that I would seduce a girl or force myself upon a woman who did not want me? I am no Kegan! No wonder you have hated me, Clarinda, if that was the kind of behaviour you thought me capable of!"

"She was – so – plausible," Clarinda murmured miserably. "She told me that she always – thought she could have been an – actress."

"And so you mean to say that we have quarrelled, fought and that you have raged at me incessantly all because some tiresome, imaginative skitter-brain beguiled you with a load of moonshine?" Lord Melburne asked her scornfully.

"I thought – I was being – loyal to my friend. I was deeply – distressed by what she – related to me."

There was a little sob in her voice and she walked towards the window.

"I would like to meet this Miss Jessica Tansley or whatever she is called now," Lord Melburne said grimly.

"You – will," Clarinda answered. "She told me – that she is coming – South for your – Wedding."

"My Wedding?" Lord Melburne flashed.

"Yes. She is a – relative of Lady Romayne and she – stayed with her in London."

There was a long silence.

Clarinda found that she was gripping her fingers so tightly together that they were almost bloodless.

"Let me make one thing absolutely clear before we embroil ourselves any further in the tangle of your friend's overactive imagination," Lord Melburne said sternly. "I am not going to marry Lady Romayne Ramsey. Kindly listen to what I am saying, Clarinda, so that there is no mistake. I have never offered for Lady Romayne and I do *not* intend to do so."

For just a moment it seemed to Clarinda that the terrible feeling of constriction round her heart was loosened. It was as if the sunshine had come out and the darkness that had seemed to encompass her ever since she had visited The Priory had vanished.

Then, as she stared out of the window so that Lord Melburne should not see her face, she heard him say,

"But I will be frank with you, Clarinda, and say that I do wish to be married. In point of fact I intend to be married very shortly."

The sunshine had gone. It seemed hardly possible that in the middle of the day a room should be so dark.

'So there *is* someone else,' Clarinda thought.

That was why he had paid no attention to her in London. He had been in love all the time with another woman.

A woman she had not met and a woman she was unaware even existed.

Now she could see all too clearly why he had not concerned himself with her save in his position as Guardian and why he had not been interested enough to seek her out alone or to ask her to dance.

He was in love, perhaps as she was in love, and this was the end of everything!

She felt that she must cry out at the misery of it, that she must run to him and ask him to hold her once more in his arms, as he had done that night he had brought her back from the caves or even to hold her hand tightly in his as he had last night when they had driven from Hetherington House to Berkeley Square.

She had clung to him, knowing the strength and warmth of his fingers, knowing that he was there beside her and knowing that once again he had rescued her from an unspeakable degradation and knowing that even in her terror she had somehow believed that he would save her as he had saved her before.

He had fought for her honour. She could see his face, savage with his anger, as he had knocked down Sir Gerald and hit him again and again. She had believed that he had done it for her own sake. Now she knew that she was just a woman who had been outraged.

There had been nothing personal in Lord Melburne's anger, only a chivalry that she had always known he had possessed and which should have made her disbelieve Jessica's mad story from the very moment she had met him.

'Once he is married I shall never see him again,' she thought despairingly.

But, as she had some remnants of pride left in her, the same pride that had prevented her from screaming and trying to escape when Nicholas had carried her away to the caves, she was able to lift her chin and say hesitatingly but quite clearly,

"I must c-congratulate – your Lordship – I hope – you will be very – happy."

Even as she said it she knew it was true. She loved him so much she wanted happiness for him even if it meant that she must be miserable and lonely for the rest of her life.

"Thank you," Lord Melburne replied quietly.

She thought that he would say more, but, because she was afraid of bursting into tears or throwing herself into his arms, she said hastily in a very small voice,

"If your Lordship is to be – married – what is to become of – me if I then have no – Guardian?"

"I thought of that as I wrote my resignation," Lord Melburne answered. "As I already told you last night, Clarinda, it is imperative that you should be married immediately."

"But there – is no one – I wish to marry," Clarinda parried quickly.

"No one?"

She shook her head. She had her back to him but she felt that he had come nearer and now she heard his voice say,

"And yet you are in love."

"How do you – know – " she began. "I mean – it is not – true."

"Clarinda, turn round and look at me."

Again she shook her head.

"N-no."

"Look at me, Clarinda," he insisted masterfully. "You don't want me to compel you?"

She remained obdurate for a moment.

Then, because she was afraid that he might touch her and her self-control would break, she turned to face him. He was nearer than she had thought.

She looked up at him and saw an expression in his eyes that made her suddenly tremble.

Quickly she looked down, her eyelashes dark on the paleness of her cheeks.

"You promised me once, Clarinda," Lord Melburne said very slowly, "that you would never lie to me. Let me ask you once again, are you in love?"

"Y-yes."

He could hardly hear her answer.

"Then surely this makes things easier," Lord Melburne remarked. "This most fortunate gentleman, whoever he may be, will become your husband and therefore will be your natural Guardian, Clarinda."

"I cannot – marry – him," Clarinda whispered.

"You mean that he has not yet asked you," Lord Melburne suggested. "That is easy, you have only to tell me who he is and if he is not on the long list of those who you have already refused, I will speak to him. I am certain that I can contrive that you are happily united within a very short space of time."

"N-no – *no*!" Clarinda cried. "Y-you don't – understand."

"What do I not understand?" he enquired in the tone of someone dealing with a difficult child.

"He – does – not care for – me."

"You are sure of that?" Lord Melburne asked.

"Quite – sure."

"I would like to be convinced of this myself," Lord Melburne said. "You have been so involved in so many tangles, Clarinda, that I just cannot trust your instinct in this. Look, for instance, at how you misunderstood me, or rather was taken in by Jessica Tansley's lies. Tell me this most enviable young man's name. I am sure without any difficulty that I can persuade him to go down on his knees in front of you."

"No – no," Clarinda pleaded, turning to the window again. "Please don't – press me, my Lord – it is something I – cannot speak about – I will be all right – and I will find myself a Guardian and someone to chaperone me. I have – no wish to be – married. I will stay at The Priory – as I always meant to do after Uncle Roderick died."

"You think you would be happy there?" Lord Melburne enquired.

"There is no need to – trouble yourself about – me, my Lord, I will arrange something."

"It does not seem to me very satisfactory," Lord Melburne remarked slowly. "You see, Clarinda, I have become tremendously involved with all your problems in these past weeks. I cannot leave you unattended and unprotected and so, before I see to my own affairs, I must find you a husband."

"I don't – want a – husband," Clarinda protested and now her voice broke on the words. "There is no one I can – marry, no one I have met in – London, so please don't think of it."

"I have thought," Lord Melburne said slowly, "although I may be mistaken, that it was someone you had met in the country, Clarinda."

For a moment Clarinda was frozen into immobility.

"What — makes you — think that?" she asked evasively, as she felt that he was waiting for an answer.

"I think I know all the men who danced attendance on you in London," Lord Melburne replied, "and yet there is somebody who has made you cry, someone you have wept for night after night. Who is he, Clarinda?"

"It is not true — who has been — telling you such things?" she asked brokenly and then she closed her eyes.

Next she gave a little gasp, for she felt his hands on her shoulders as he turned her round to face him.

"Must you go on lying?" he asked. "Look at me, Clarinda!"

For a moment she resisted him before she opened her eyes filled with tears and looked into his.

"My poor, unhappy little love," he said softly. "I am a brute to tease you, but you have made me suffer so excruciatingly these past weeks that I wanted to punish you just a little."

For a few moments she could only stare at him, tears blinding her eyes, feeling that she must be dreaming.

"Do you really think that I could marry anyone else?" Lord Melburne asked, "or let you marry anyone but me?"

"What are you — saying to — me?" Clarinda whispered.

There was a strange excited feeling tingling over her, a feeling that made her tremble, but not with fear.

"I am trying to tell you, my dearest sweetest heart, that I love you and you have driven me nearly insane. I don't think any man should have to go through the torture you have made me suffer these past few weeks, when I have watched every man you met dangling after you, proposing to you, wanting to love you, while I dared not even look at you."

"You ignored – me," she whispered. "You never – spoke to me, you never – asked me to – dance."

"Do you not realise, my foolish love," he asked, "that if I had so much as touched you I would have taken you in my arms and kissed you as I kissed you once before. It has been an inexpressible agony to see you looking so beautiful and to know that you were not for me."

His fingers tightened on her shoulders until they hurt.

"Just how could you built that impossible ridiculous barrier between us? I have walked about my room night after night saying the words 'Jessica Tansley? Jessica Tansley?' until I think they are engraved on my heart. I thought that she must have meant something in my past and yet my memory was blank. She stood like an angel with a flaming torch between me and my only hope of happiness. Clarinda, how could you be such a nitwit as to believe her?"

"Forgive me – please – forgive me."

Her eyes were looking up at his, her lips were parted a little and her breath was coming quickly between them and, because she looked so entrancingly lovely, he gave a little sound that was half a groan, half a cry of triumph and then swept her closely and crushingly into his arms.

His lips were on hers and he kissed her wildly and passionately with the desperation of a man who thought he had lost all that mattered most to him in the world.

When, after a long time, he raised his head it was to look down into her face, flushed and glowing with a radiance that he had never seen before.

"I love you," he said hoarsely. "*Oh, God, how I love you*! And to think that it was only last night after you had left me that I decided I must go abroad."

"Go abroad!" she cried. "But why?"

"Because I could not bear to be near you any longer and not hold you like this, not kiss you and not beg you to marry me," he answered. "Can you not understand, Clarinda, what I have been through, wanting you, thinking that my love was in vain and believing you spoke the truth when you said you hated me?"

"I don't think that I ever hated you after I came to know you. And then I – loved you – I loved you – so much that I was – afraid of myself."

"And yet you remained loyal to that idiotic, deceitful over-imaginative friend of yours?"

"I thought you did not – love me," Clarinda replied. "I thought I should find myself like all the other women who loved you, who found you – irresistible and who – bored you."

She shivered and looked into his face.

"I am afraid that – I too might bore you?"

He tightened his hold on her so violently that she cried out with the pain of it.

"You are never to think of such a thing," he said fiercely. "It is impossible that we shall ever be bored with each other and I will tell you why."

He kissed her forehead.

"First, my darling, because you have such an exciting brain, although Grandmama thinks it is most regrettable.

It will I do know keep us talking, arguing and perhaps even quarrelling occasionally for the rest of our lives."

He bent and kissed her eyes.

"Secondly, my most adorable one, you have already mapped out a programme that will keep me occupied for years. Because of you I intend to go into Politics and if as a Politician's wife you complain that you have too much to do, it will be entirely your own fault."

He kissed her lips before she could reply and then, close against her mouth, he said,

"Lastly, my lovely one, I adore you as I have never adored anyone in the whole of my life. I never knew that love could be like this. I have never felt for any woman what I feel for you. I think that for every man, there is in his heart a shrine where he places his ideal woman. You are in my shrine, Clarinda, and there you will remain. My love, my guide and inspiration and most important of all, my wife!"

He sought her lips and his kiss was gentle and had something reverent in it.

Then he asked her softly,

"Is that what you want of me, Clarinda?"

"You know it is," she whispered. "You know all I want is your love – because Buck, I love – you until there is – nothing left in the world – but my love for you – I cannot think of anything else. I only know that – my heart belongs to your – heart and I want to be – married to you – and to belong to you."

"How soon will you marry me?" Lord Melburne asked. "Tonight?"

"H-how could – w-we?" Clarinda stammered.

"Very easily," he answered. "Grandmama said something only this morning that made me hope that you did not hate me as much as I feared. So before I left London I obtained a Special Licence."

"Oh, how – wonderful!" Clarinda breathed.

"Then shall we be married later this evening in the Private Chapel?" he asked.

"I want – more than anything in the world – to be your wife," Clarinda answered, "and – to be – safe."

"You will always be safe in my arms, my darling. There will be no more terror, no more fears for you by night or by day. You will be close to me and if any man so much as looks at you, I swear I will kill him. You are mine, do you hear me? *Mine!*"

His arms tightened about her and his lips, passionate, masterful and possessive, captured hers.

The whole world seemed to be filled with sunshine and celestial music, which swept them into a Heaven all of their own.

They were now one person, close, united and joined by a love that Clarinda knew would be with them forever and ever in this life and many other lives yet to come.

When he then raised his head, Lord Melburne saw that her eyelids were for the first time heavy with the passion he had aroused in her and deep in her eyes there was a flame that echoed the fire in his.

"Oh, my wonderful glorious darling," she whispered tremulously, her breath coming quickly between her lips. "It is not very original – but I find you – irresistible."

"Is that not lucky?" he replied, his voice was deep with desire, but she heard a hint of laughter in it, "because, my beloved adorable sweetheart, I find you completely irresistible too!"

OTHER BOOKS IN THIS SERIES

The Barbara Cartland Eternal Collection is the unique opportunity to collect all five hundred of the timeless beautiful romantic novels written by the world's most celebrated and enduring romantic author.

Named the Eternal Collection because Barbara's inspiring stories of pure love, just the same as love itself, the books will be published on the internet at the rate of four titles per month until all five hundred are available.

The Eternal Collection, classic pure romance available worldwide for all time.